TRANSLATIONS OF THE CARNIVAL
COMEDIES OF HANS SACHS (1494-1576)

Translated and Edited by

Robert Aylett

The Edwin Mellen Press
Lewiston/Queenston/Lampeter

Library of Congress Cataloging-in-Publication Data

Sachs, Hans, 1494-1576.
    [Fastnachtspiele. English. Selections]
    Translations of the Carnival comedies of Hans Sachs (1494-1576) /
translated and edited by Robert Aylett.
        p.   cm.
    Includes bibliographical references.
    ISBN 0-7734-1342-1
    I. Aylett, Robert. II. Title. III. Series.
PT1767.E5A95   1994
832'.4--dc20   94-17946
                                                            CIP

This is volume 4 in the continuing series
Bristol German Publications
Volume 4 ISBN 0-7734-1342-1
BCP Series ISBN 0-7734-1360-X

A CIP catalog record for this book is available from the British Library.

Copyright © 1994 The Edwin Mellen Press

All rights reserved. For information contact

The Edwin Mellen Press
Box 450
Lewiston, New York
USA 14092-0450

The Edwin Mellen Press
Box 67
Queenston, Ontario
CANADA L0S 1L0

The Edwin Mellen Press, Ltd.
Lampeter, Dyfed, Wales
UNITED KINGDOM SA48 7DY

Printed in Great Britain by
Antony Rowe Ltd, Chippenham, Wiltshire

TRANSLATIONS OF THE CARNIVAL COMEDIES OF HANS SACHS (1494-1576)

This book is dedicated to two people not destined to meet:
my father, Reginald Aylett, who died in 1972
and
my daughter, Anna Katharina Friedmann-Aylett, born in 1986.

They might have enjoyed Sachs together.

CONTENTS

TABLE OF ILLUSTRATIONS

The illustrations used throughout this volume are taken, with the kind permission of **Hans Carl Verlag**, from the exhibition catalogue *Die Welt des Hans Sachs. 400 Holzschnitte des 16. Jahrhunderts (Ausstellungskataloge der Stadtgeschichtlichen Museen Nürnberg, 10)*, 1976.

1. INTRODUCTION

This translated selection of Hans Sachs's carnival comedies or *Fastnachtspiele* was prompted by a variety of considerations. Two of them are, or were, of an appropriately celebratory nature. The first is the imminence of Sachs's 500th birthday (he was born on 5 November 1494), an occasion which German scholars in this country should not allow to pass unacknowledged, despite, or perhaps precisely because of, Sachs's having nowadays somewhat slipped into the margins of many degree programmes in German. The second was the recent celebration by Goldsmiths' College of the centenary of its founding: an event which, not surprisingly in an institution so deeply committed to the performing arts, involved numerous performances of music and drama. The German section of the Department of European Languages was invited to contribute to the festivities. Sachs's name somehow emerged, and a decision was taken to perform at least one *Fastnachtspiel* in a new English version for the benefit of the widest possible audience. The 'Vita Brevis' company duly performed *The Doctor with the Big Nose* in the College's central courtyard, on a raised lawn, within thirty yards of the barbecue and bar, to a partly itinerant, partly seated audience, who received the piece with gratifying warmth.

Subsequent conversations with colleagues who witnessed the spectacle encouraged me to think that not only were Sachs's carnival

comedies still an appealing form of entertainment in the right
circumstances, but that they also comprised useful material for
dramaturgical study and also a rich source of information about historical
circumstances and social attitudes, in short, the socio-economic realities of
certain areas of early-to-mid sixteenth-century life. It seemed a natural step
to make more texts available to the broad constituency of those potentially
interested but who would find the original German a barrier to
understanding. This would not, of course, exclude students of German,
although it would be a matter of considerable regret to me if students of
German ceased to bother with the original precisely because an English
version of Sachs had become available.

I refer to 'an English version' rather than to a 'translation' for a
number of reasons. Most of us who earn a living at least in part by
teaching the German language to undergraduates will be familiar with the
problems of marking translation work. Should pedestrian accuracy be
deemed more meritorious than slightly wayward flair? How does one
render the 'feel' of a passage? How are proverbs to be translated? What
does one do when faced with the realisation that, on occasion, the German
mind conceives of things quite differently from the English mind, and there
is sometimes no satisfactory match between the two languages? In the
bleakest moments, student and teacher alike realise that the innocent-
looking instruction 'Translate into English' is little more than an invitation
to affirm that our post-Babel affliction is indeed irremediable. Informed,
heartened indeed, by the parallel realisation that the above instruction is
merely a request to interpret, or to 'do into' another tongue, or to write
what an English thinker might have thought or said in the circumstances,
had it occurred to him or her to do so, students continue pragmatically to
render one language into another and to produce good working versions
of selected passages. This I have tried to do in the case of Sachs's carnival
comedies: to produce versions of the plays which do them justice, which

render their thoughts, their spirit, and their form, rather than providing a dictionary-accurate translation of their every word, and which attempt to convey their vibrant mood and their dynamic qualities in an attempt to lift them out of the rather dusty and under-used pigeon-hole where they seem to have landed.

Sachs wrote some 85 *Fastnachtspiele*, or at least in his *Generalregister* of 1560 described that number of dramas in that way. Researchers have diligently reduced this number since, disqualifying texts which Sachs had elsewhere labelled differently, or which seem not to conform to the broad pattern of the *Fastnachtspiel* as defined by academic research. [1] Be that as it may, to select nine for translation, as is the case here, is to leave out a good number of familiar and excellent works, notably *Das kelberbruten (1551)*, *Der krämerskorb (1554)*, the *Neidhart* plays, the *Eulenspiegel* plays, *Der roßdieb zw Fünsing (1553)*, *Das narrenschneiden (1537)*, *Das hoffgsindt veneris (1517)*, and *Der pawr inn dem fegfewer (1552)*, to name but a few. The present selection contains works of sufficient merit to replace those listed; one of the selection criteria employed was certainly to bring to the attention of a wider audience relatively neglected works such as *Der ketzermeister mit den vil kessel suppen (1553)*, or *Das weynent hündlein (1554)*, which seem not to have featured in previously published selections of Sachs in German, and have never, to my knowledge, been put into English. Other criteria were: to provide a thematic cross-section of the *Fastnachtspiele*; to select plays based on a wide variety of sources; to select texts which themselves reveal noteworthy aspects of the socio-economic realities of their age; and to assemble a collection which affords readers and audiences the opportunity to appreciate the dynamic quality of the *Fastnachtspiel* genre, with its combination of pithy language, simple visual qualities, fast-moving action, and warm appreciation of the frailties of the

---

[1] Both E. Catholy and E. Geiger would wish to reduce the number of 'genuine' articles to 77. See B. Könnecker, *Hans Sachs* (Sammlung Metzler 94), Stuttgart, 1971, p. 62.

4

human condition.

May I take this occasion to express my thanks to all colleagues at Goldsmiths' College who supported me in this project, particularly those who, in its early stages, listened to or read their way through sheaves of at times dreadful doggerel; to Dr. Christopher Southgate, of Exeter University, for providing a poet's eye; and above all to Professor Peter Skrine, of Bristol University, for wise advice and much encouragement.

2. HANS SACHS: LITERATURE TO THE LAST

Much of what we know about Sachs comes from the lengthy poem 'Summa all meiner gedicht' ('The Sum of my Writings'), written in 1566-67, almost ten years before he died. It was printed in 1576, under the more grandiose title of *Valete, Des Weitberhümbten Teutschen Poeten Hans Sachsen zu Nürnberg / Darinn er selbs / im 71. Jar seines alters / sein leben und inhalt / anzal und ordnung aller seiner Gedicht / reimenweiß verfaßt / gestelt und beschriben / im Jar nach Christi geburt 1567.* [1] Other works of his provide incidental details, and further information may be gleaned from official documents relating to his business and artistic activities and kept in the city archives at Nürnberg. Fundamentally, though, little is known about Sachs's life other than via his literary activities.

He was born in the perhaps unpropitious-sounding, but actually rather well-to-do Kotgasse (now Brunnengasse), in Nuremberg, on 5 November, 1494. His father Jorg (Georg) was a tailor who moved to the

---

[1] *A farewell from the widely renowned German poet Hans Sachs, from Nuremberg, in which, in the 71st year of his life, he has compiled and set down in verse the details of his life, and the number and sequence of his poetic works, in the year 1567 A.D.*

Unless otherwise indicated, all references to Sachs's works are to A. von Keller and E. Goetze, *Hans Sachs*, 26 Vols, Tübingen, 1870-1908. Here, Vol. 24, p.203.

city from Zwickau and married Christina Prunner, the widow of a master tailor. The house where Sachs was born had belonged to his mother before her second marriage. Sachs saw the light of the world some two years after Columbus had led the way to America, when Nuremberg, already a well-established city, was set to profit further from the opening up of the new world. Not only was Nuremberg located on the old East-West trade routes, but also on the North-South routes, an important factor given that the centre of trade and finances in Europe was to shift from the Mediterranean to the Atlantic coast over the coming years. The city contributed significantly to the opening up of the world, with Regiomontanus providing mathematical expertise and Behaim constructing among the earliest of globes; and it was an early centre of Humanism and the propagation of the arts, with Albrecht Dürer perhaps its most notable resident of the epoch. [2]

Sachs was, it seems, fortunate to survive infancy: but a plague epidemic left him untouched, and he went on to live to an immense age. Between the ages of seven and fifteen, Sachs attended a Latin school (the *Spitalschule*), where he received a grounding in reading, writing, and mathematics; later he learnt grammar, geography, and singing. He was then apprenticed to a master cobbler, and at this time began to learn the art of the *Meistergesang* ('master-song') at the hands of Lienhardt Nunnenbeck, a noted practitioner at a time when the barber-surgeon Hans Folz, a major contributor to the tradition of the Nuremberg *Fastnachtspiel*, was leader of the city's singing school. *Meistergesang* was not a truly popular form of song: it was controlled, regulated, and formalised by an urban 'middle' class.

When, in 1511, Sachs embarked on the obligatory travelling phase

---

[2]For a most informative discussion of the nature and role of the city of Nürnberg during this period, see P. Broadhead, 'Self-Interest and Security: Relations between Nuremberg and its Territory in the Early Sixteenth Century', in *German History*, Vol. 11, No. 1, pp. 1-19.

of his apprenticeship, his path took him for the most part along major routes to cities and towns with singing schools, and he was thus able to combine his two chief interests while absent from Nuremberg. He journeyed through Bavaria, many parts of modern Austria, and along the Rhine. In 1513, he arrived at Wels, where it is believed that he started to write his own material in the form of love-songs, and where he became familiar with a translated version of Boccaccio's *Decameron*, on which he was later to draw for certain of his *Fastnachtspiele*. It was in Munich, however, in 1514-15, where Sachs wrote his first *Meisterlieder*; he also played an active role in the city's singing school. In May 1515, Sachs returned briefly to Nuremberg, but journeyed onwards to Würzburg and to Frankfurt, where again he sought involvement with the singing school, helping supervise activities.

Sachs returned home in 1516, having gained considerable experience as an apprentice cobbler and as a lay artist - and, perhaps just as important, experience of combining these two aspects of his life. The gift from his parents of the house and workshop in the Kotgasse was to ease any material worries, and naturally facilitated Sachs's leading a double life of master cobbler and committed man of letters. His first collection of *Meisterlieder* appeared in the years 1516-18; he became a Meister (master) in the singing school in 1518; and in 1519 he married the seventeen-year-old Kunigunde Kreuzer, a reasonably well-to-do young woman. In a very few years Sachs had become a married man of property, and by 1520 was a master of his trade, and a leading contributor to singing activities in Nuremberg.

From his Marxist point of view, Wedler sees in Sachs a member of the bourgeois opposition frustrating the popular struggle for emancipation being played out in these highly-charged early years of the Lutheran revolution: a far cry, then, from being a representative of the peasants and plebeians, of the 'common man'. [3] Whatever the merits of Wedler's analysis, it would seem that the purchase by the Sachs family of a second house, in 1522, and the production of two daughters by 1523, provide evidence of a life not exactly fraught with hardship.

Intellectually, Sachs became very much engaged with Luther's works during this period, and with *Die wittembergisch nachtigall* (*The Nightingale of Wittemberg, July 1523*) made a major literary impact. [4] Championing Luther and the cause of the peasants, and highly critical of the princes and bishops, the work represents a decisive move towards the realm of political literature. It went into numerous reprints, and naturally enough attracted much odium from those who felt attacked, explicitly or implicitly, including some of the city fathers of Nuremberg, who feared it might stir up the lower classes. Sachs occupied an uneasy middle ground: he was of the establishment, by virtue of his civic status, yet apparently propagating ideas calculated to appeal to the revolutionary instincts of the poor and deprived. His anti-Catholic position becomes even clearer in 1524 with the appearance of the *Disputation zwischen einem chorherrn und schuchmacher* (*Disputation Between a Canon and a Cobbler*). [5] Here, as in other contemporary works by Sachs, we see portrayed the intellectual victory of the Lutheran or evangelical 'common man' over the corrupt defenders of the Catholic church, and we hear voiced legitimate complaints about the existing socio-economic and political order. Yet whilst Sachs seems to be sailing close to the wind of the peasant revolt, the reality was that, like Luther, he was not an advocate of any sort of overthrowing of the social order: such an action would offend against God's ordained pattern of things. The civic authorities took another view, and began to watch Sachs's

---

[3] K. Wedler, *Hans Sachs*, Reclam, Leipzig, 1976, pp. 47 ff.

[4] Keller and Goetze, Vol. 6, pp. 368-86. The introduction to the piece is found in Keller and Goetze, Vol. 22, pp. 3-5.

[5] Keller and Goetze, Vol. 22, pp. 6-33.

literary activities closely, believing they had found in him a *Schwärmer* or *Täufer*. But far from being such a visionary zealot, Sachs was essentially conservative - as we shall see from his carnival comedies, which frequently deal with disorder, but ultimately strive to reassert normality.

By 1526-27, Sachs was widely read and had developed into a many-sided writer: from song to tragedy, from prose debates to carnival comedy. His continued apparent advocacy of political and social change now brought him into conflict with the Nuremberg authorities. Sachs was publicly censured, ostensibly for publishing materials without permission, but no doubt also because of the content of the work in question, a collaborative effort with Andreas Osiander, a leading Nuremberg advocate of the Reformation: the *Auslegung der wunderlichen weissagung von dem papstum* (Interpretation of the Peculiar Papal Prophecy) was trenchant in its condemnation of the Pope. [6]

Not surprisingly, Sachs spent the years 1527-28 in composing relatively uncontroversial *Meisterlieder*, and was deemed rehabilitated with his *Lobspruch der statt Nürnberg (Eulogy on the City of Nuremberg)* [7] which appeared as Charles V was installed as Holy Roman Emperor. There followed a period of enormous output: by July 1531 Sachs had produced his third volume of *Meisterlieder*, and had numerous tragedies, comedies, and epigrammatic and aphoristic poems to his name. In 1531, his father died; Sachs himself had, by then, fathered five sons and two daughters, not all of whom had survived.

In 1533, the tradition of *Fastnachtspiel* was revived in Nürnberg, and this seems to have offered Sachs a new direction: away from the overtly political and theological tone of many of his earlier works, and towards a humorous concern with everyday issues, where he could demonstrate his

---

[6]Keller and Goetze, Vol. 22, pp. 131-36.

[7]Keller and Goetze, Vol. 4, pp. 189-99.

real understanding of what makes people tick. Yet his carnival comedies do not essentially deal with real people: nearly all the figures on stage are representative types or caricatures, who afford access to the common elements of humanity and social living. It may thus be argued that Sachs's shifting of interest from the realm of European politics, in order to enter the domestic world of carnival comedy, does not represent an intellectual descent, for it is in the latter realm that he explores the abstract essentials of the human condition, rising above the temporary manifestations of social and ecclesiastical politics.

Some ten *Fastnachtspiele* appeared between 1533 and 1539; in June 1538 he completed a third volume of epigrammatic poetry; and in November 1538 he started his fifth volume of *Meisterlieder*. From 1539 onwards, however, external events dictated that Sachs was to return to the sphere of more public political writing. *Die gemartert Theologia* (*Theology Martyred*) of March 1539 [8] revives anti-papist sentiments, whilst other writings of this period express anti-feudal and anti-capitalist thoughts. Sachs talks of the urgent need for reform, lest the common people should suffer even further, but still, characteristically, falls short of advocating overthrowing an unjust social and economic system. By 1542, Sachs was in a position to purchase another house - whilst keeping the old parental home in the Kotgasse - financing the purchase from the sale of other properties. It is perhaps clear why Sachs should, on the one hand, rail against injustice, but, on the other, advocate a quietistic acceptance of the given order of things.

The following years saw, among a great variety of works concerned with contemporary events, the completion of an eighth book of *Meisterlieder*, and an epitaph for Martin Luther, who died in 1546. A significant development in terms of Sachs's already broad creative range

---

[8]Keller and Goetze, Vol. 1, pp. 338-44.

was his increasing use of material borrowed from Boccaccio and from German *Schwankbücher* (popular collections of short farcical stories, anecdotes, and pranks).

Whether as a response to the dangers of publicly engaging in political debate, [9] or as a result of evolving natural inclination, Sachs now moved more towards the *Fastnachtspiel*, and its more generalised, humorous analysis of the human condition, and used these new source materials freely. By 1550-51, Sachs's output of drama had increased considerably, with the *Fastnachtspiel* beginning to dominate the other forms, namely, comedy and tragedy, although the balance was to be redressed in the later years of this decade. But even these carnival comedies were not free from interference and indeed censorship: *Der Abt im wildpad* (*The Abbot in the Thermal Spa*) of December 1550 was performed twice in January 1551 and then banned for its anti-catholic content. Of the plays in the present collection, four come from the period 1550-51, three from 1553-54, and two from 1559. All reflect a blend of caricature and realism which allows Sachs to paint, albeit with a broad brush, real, everyday problems, be they political, financial, or more personal: problems which, whilst they may distantly have echoed the major theological and political problems besetting Europe, are of immediate concern in a domestic situation.

By now, Sachs was complaining of the onset of old age, [10] but was active in preparing the folio edition of his works. His wife, Kunigunde, died in March 1560: the two had been married for forty-one years, and none of their seven children survived Kunigunde, although their daughter Katharina

---

[9]K. Wedler, *Hans Sachs*, Leipzig, 1976, p. 157, draws attention to an imperial banning of anti-papal literature in 1548.

[10]*Ein klag-gesprech uber das schwer alter* (*A Lamentation on the Hardships of Old Age*), Keller and Goetze, Vol. 7, pp. 211-19. This is dated by Sachs as being written on his birthday in 1558, although Keller and Goetze place it one year earlier (see Vol. 25, p. 521).

had left four grandchildren. After this sad event, Sachs virtually gave up his trade, and seems also to have given up any active involvement in staging *Fastnachtspiele*.

In September 1561, at the age of sixty-seven years, Sachs remarried. His new wife, Barbara Harscher, was a twenty-seven-year-old widow, and mother of six children. His creative writing flourished, but Sachs gave up his activities at the singing school. At the turn of 1561-62, Sachs and his new wife survived what was, for Sachs, his second experience of a plague epidemic. This he described in detail in the prologue to the fourth volume of his collected works. In 1562, Sachs wrote one of his most intimately personal love poems, 'Das künstlich frawen-lob' ('In artful praise of woman'), dedicated to his new wife. In 1566-67 he draws up the 'Summa all meiner Gedicht', embracing a total of over 6,000 titles; in 1568, he composes the accompanying verses to Jost (or Jobst) Amman's illustrations in his *Ständebuch*. [11] By 1573, Sachs had ceased writing, and he died on 19 January 1576, at the age of eighty-one.

Sachs's literary output was massive. In terms of numbers, his carnival comedies, numbering less than one hundred, cannot compare with other genres. They do represent, however, a significant element in his works, and in terms of quality are splendid manifestations of his witty appreciation of human folly and of the everyday issues affecting the common man, as we shall see.

---

[11]Jost Amman, *Eygentliche Beschreibung aller Stände auff Erden...*, 1568 (*A True Description of all Trades*). For details see: Keller and Goetze, Vol. 24, p. 202. The verses composed by Sachs appear in Keller and Goetze, Vol. 23, pp. 271-303.

3. SACHS IN ENGLISH

1. Previous translations

There have been numerous English versions of individual works by Sachs, and some collections. It would seem that the earliest work 'translated out of ye Germayne tongue into Englysshe' was by **Anthony Scoloker** in 1548: his *Goodly dysputacion betwene a Christen shomaker / and a Popysshe Parson with two other parsones more, done within the famous Citie of Norembourgh* is, of course, Sachs's *Disputation zwischen einem Chorherren und Schuchmacher darin das wort gottes und ein recht Christlich wesen verfochten wurdt (1524),* though given the ordering of the English title and the extra details it contains it seems likely that Scoloker worked from a Dutch version, *Een schoon disputatie van eenen Euangelischen Schoenmaker.* [1] This near-contemporary work apart, Sachs inspired little further interest among English translators until the twentieth century, when in 1903 **W. H. H. Chambers** led the way with his version of Sachs's *Fastnachtspiel Der farent schueler mit dem deufel pannen (1551),* translated

---

[1] See Keller and Goetze, Vol. 24, pp. 80-82, and also Vol. 22, p. 6 footnote for the reference concerning Herford's discussion of this point.

as *Raising the Devil*, but rendered into prose rather than into verse. [2]

W. Leighton, in 1910, claims to have 'first done into English verse' a selection of 'merry tales', and three 'Shrovetide plays'. [3] The latter are *The Travelling Scholar from Paradise, The Horse Thief*, and *The Hot Iron*, being respectively versions of *Der farent schueler ins paradeiß (1550), Der roßdieb zw Fünsing mit den thollen diebischen bawren (1553)* and *Das heiß eisen (1551)*. Leighton is apparently justified in his claim. Some time elapses before **S. A.** Eliot offers *The Wandering Scholar from Paradise*, in 1922. [4] **H. G.** Atkins follows in 1926 with the verse translation *The Farmer in Purgatory (Der pawr im fegfewer, 1552)*, coupled with his own pastiche *The Student in Purgatory*. [5] **J.** Krumpelmann adds to the list in 1927 with his *Brooding Calves. A Shrovetide Play with Three Persons*, which is a verse translation of *Das kelberbruten (1551)*. [6] A major contribution is made by **E. U.** Ouless in 1930, with his *Seven Shrovetide Plays*. [7] As well as the familiar *Wandering Scholar*, this collection includes unique translations such as *Five Poor Travellers (Die fünff armen wanderer, 1539), Dame Truth (Fraw warheit mit dem paurn/Frau warheyt*

---

[2]*Raising the Devil: a Shrove-tide or Carnival Play. (Der farent schueler mit dem deufel pannen; ain Fasnacht Spil) of Hans Sachs. Translated by W. H. H. Chambers*, in A. Bates, *The Drama*, London, 1903, pp. 171-80.

[3]W. Leighton, *Merry Tales and Three Shrovetide Plays by Hans Sachs, now first done into English verse*, London, 1910. Reprinted in *Library of World Literature* Series, Connecticut, 1978.

[4]*The Wandering Scholar from Paradise. A Fastnachtspiel with Three Persons*, Adapted by Samuel A. Eliot Jr., in *Little Theatre Classics, Vol. 4*, Boston, 1922, pp. 115-37, and also in: B. H. Clark (ed.), *World Drama*, New York, 1933, pp. 365-70.

[5]H. G. Atkins, *The Farmer in Purgatory, translated from the German of Hans Sachs - Der Bauer im Fegfeuer, 1552; and the Student in Purgatory*, London, 1926.

[6]*Brooding Calves; Shrovetide Play with Three Persons*. Translated from the German by John Krumpelmann, in *Poet-Lore*, xxxviii, 1927, pp. 435-46.

[7]E. U. Ouless, *Seven Shrovetide Plays, translated and adapted from the German of Hans Sachs*, London, 1930.

will niemandt herbergen, 1550), and *Death in the Tree (Der Todt im stock, 1555).* [8] One of the translations, *The Children of Eve: A Morality,* was also published elsewhere. [9] Soon after this, in 1935, we have **P. Wayne's** *The Strolling Clerk from Paradise,* [10] itself closely followed by **B. Q. Morgan's** three 'Shrovetide comedies' published in 1937: [11] *The Scholar Bound for Paradise, The Merchant's Basket (Der krämerskorb, 1554),* and *The Hot Iron.*

At this stage, interest seems to wane once more, probably as a result of international events. A single work is published in the 1940s, *Das walt got: A Meisterlied,* which appeared in 1941, translated by **F. H. Ellis.** [12] Nothing more is published until the appearance in 1950 of **B. A. Hunter's** *Who'll Carry the Bag?,* another version of the *Krämerskorb.* [13] The most recent works in translating Sachs would seem to be **B. A. Rifkin's** *The Book of Trades* [14] and **I. E. Clark's** *Hans Sachs: The Narrenschneiden. A Mardi-*

---

[8]*Die fünff armen wanderer,* Keller and Goetze, Vol. 9, pp. 12-22; *Frau warheit mit dem paurn,* Keller and Goetze, Vol. 14, pp. 99-110; *Der Todt im stock,* Keller and Goetze, Vol. 11, pp. 451-61.

[9]*The Children of Eve: a Morality.* Translated and adapted by E. U. Ouless, in C. M. Martin (ed.), *Fifty One-Act Plays,* London, 1934, pp. 949-60. (*Wie gott, der herr, Adam unnd Eva ihre kinder segnet, 1553,* Keller and Goetze, Vol. 11, pp. 386-99).

[10]*The Strolling Clerk from Paradise, by Hans Sachs.* English by Philip Wayne, in P. Wayne, *One-Act Comedies,* London, 1935, pp. 45-62, and also London (OUP), 1935.

[11]B. Q. Morgan, *The Scholar Bound for Paradise; The Merchant's Basket; The Hot Iron. Three Shrovetide Comedies translated from Hans Sachs,* Stanford University (Microfilm), 1937.

[12]*Das walt Got: A Meisterlied.* With Introduction, Commentary, and Bibliography [and Translation] by F. H. Ellis (*Hans Sachs Studies, 1*), Bloomington, 1941.

[13] B. A. Hunter, *Who'll Carry the Bag? A Comedy after the Kremerkorb of Hans Sachs,* 1950, (no place of publication).

[14]*The Book of Trades, Ständebuch. [Woodcuts by] Jost Amman and [text by] Hans Sachs.* With a new introduction by B. A. Rifkin, New York, 1973. Two further versions of this text exist from the 1930s: *A True Description of All Trades; published in Frankfort in the year 1568, with six of the illustrations by Jobst (sic) Amman,* Brooklyn, 1930; and *A True Description of All Trades. First published in the year 1568. With six of the illustrations relating to the art of printing by Jobst (sic) Amman,* Eugene, Oregon, 1939. See also Keller and Goetze, Vol. 24, p. 202.

gras Play, [15] which seems to be essentially a director's script. Significantly, nothing seems to have been published in England for some 60 years.

It is the carnival comedies or Shrovetide plays, then, which have attracted most attention from translators, although the range represented is far from wide. All of the various translations have their merits and demerits, some solving certain problems better than others. In briefly examining a number of these older translations, certain of the problems attached to putting German sixteenth-century verse drama into an English equivalent may be illustrated. Where attention is drawn to weaker moments, it is not from any sense of superiority on the part of the present translator, who, having refrained from comparing his efforts with those of earlier translators until completing his task, found many delightful and instructive moments in these earlier works.

In his *Merry Tales and Three Shrovetide Plays by Hans Sachs, now first done into English verse,* William Leighton furnishes an introduction from which we learn that:

> Though absolutely ignorant of all the rules of dramatic art, Hans Sachs had wonderful dramatic inspirations, which made his plays successful by the mere force of his simple lines of characterization. He was a natural dramatist, producing a great number of plays which were highly satisfactory to his neighbours and countrymen, especially the Shrovetide Plays, which were frequently humorous little glimpses of peasant life. There are no considerations of time or place in these little dramas, no stage illusions. Considerable lapses of time occur without any intimation to reader or audience except what may be gathered from the words of the actors; and all the characters are presented in one place where often, under the circumstances of the story, they could not possibly be; locations and times of events being changed indiscriminately throughout the one-act play in a very puzzling manner. (p. xii f.)

---

[15]*Hans Sachs: The Narrenschneiden. A Mardi-gras Play.* Translated from the German by I. E. Clark (no date, published by the author).

and also that:

> His Pegasus, perhaps, never soared over the loftiest heights of
> Olympus; but he did not wish it to do so; he did what was better:
> he employed his poetic genius to help, instruct, make easier and
> more cheerful, the lives of his neighbours; and, by guiding his muse
> in this way, he fully deserved his immortality. (p. xv)

There is much here to stimulate argument, but it is difficult to come to
terms with Leighton's patronising tone. As is the case with the introduction,
the translation itself veers between the competent and the rather
unsatisfactory, as can be seen when the fluently attractive opening lines
from *The Hot Iron* are compared with the stultifying woodenness of the
closing lines:

Wife: Four years ago at marriage vow
             My husband was more dear than now.
             How has the love that then I knew
             Burned out? The love, that once was true,
             Quite gone! It is a mystery.
             [..............................]

Cousin: Think never more of iron test;
             In faithful love let hope now rest.
             Hot iron much of kindness lacks;
             Try not such test; so says Hans Sachs.

Leighton's performance is most uneven, and it seems he finds the twin
demands of conforming to rhyme and metrical patterns occasionally
irksome. Naturalness - the very quality identified as likely to commend
Sachs's works to his 'neighbours and countrymen' - is frequently sacrificed.
Of course, verse cannot pretend to be the natural medium for conveying
everyday speech, but any translation of Sachs's verse *into verse* should at
least aim to be as unstilted as the original, and Leighton often fails in this
respect.

    Despite identifying in his introduction an occasionally puzzling lack of stage directions and notes in the originals, Leighton generally resists the temptation to insert fresh stage directions and to 'improve' the dramas in this respect. His language strikes the modern reader as generally a little stiff, bordering on the mannered and perhaps mock-archaic at times, when he uses 'thee' and 'thou', 'list', and 'pother'. 'E'en' and 'ne'er', when used, seem expedient elisions. On occasion, Leighton falls between two stools, giving a literal translation and adding a footnote to say that a good idiomatic translation would be desirable, as on p. 263 (*The Hot Iron*), where 'I must give back the cow' is footnoted with: 'Idiom for taking back an accusation'.

There are, nonetheless, moments in Leighton's translations which do commend his work: a good example is found in the closing lines of *The Travelling Scholar from Paradise*:

Farmer: Who falls a victim to deceit
                 Should not find fault when others meet
                 The like misfortune; but forgive,
                 That all in peacefulness may live:
                 'Kind charity for faulty acts
                 Redeems our own', remarks Hans Sachs.

Eliot's *The Wandering Scholar from Paradise* is of considerable interest in that, unlike Leighton's work, it contains copious stage directions not present in the original, a number of which give precise instructions to the actors regarding gestures they are to use to underline their reactions to each other. Thus the wife is 'moved to tears' (p. 366); she is seen to be 'getting an idea'; and she acts 'beseechingly'. The student in the same conversation strikes 'a thoughtful attitude, finger to forehead, and eyeing her under his brows'; he cocks his hat 'with a graphic gesture'; he nods 'reassuringly'; and he starts 'glancing about for the new husband'. Elsewhere, Eliot seeks to interpret - for the benefit of the actors or perhaps for the reader? - what the characters are feeling or thinking. The wife is 'surprised at the suggestion from him, accepting it eagerly' (p. 367), whilst her husband 'starts violently, clutching the stocking like a bludgeon, but controls himself; and she goes on quite unaware'.

One of the effects of Eliot's inserting non-original directions of this sort is undoubtedly to encourage an acting style perhaps more appropriate to mime or indeed to silent film than to the stage: the conveying of thought and feeling solely via a body language reliant on exaggerated gesture. But Eliot's additions go beyond merely suggesting an acting style. More seriously, the directions themselves constitute an interpretation of the play, and constrain actors to follow that interpretation, a feature much less in evidence in the originals. Spontaneity, improvisation, natural wit, a working out of the action from the virtually bare text - essential elements in the art of acting - are discouraged by Eliot: yet these would seem to be highly desirable qualities in the realm of *Fastnachtspiel* and its presentation, where performances, as we know, took place and still do take place in what for mainstream modern theatrical conventions - street and pub theatre apart - are relatively makeshift circumstances, with minimal props and, perhaps inevitably, much interplay between the audience and the actors. [16] In adding so many directions, Eliot seems to be attempting to fix the delivery of the text once and for all, which is surely contrary to the spirit and nature of the Fastnachtspiel, and attempting to offer, via the stage directions, a way of understanding the text and the characters. He is dictating, in other words, the audience's reaction and their understanding of the play.

The quality of Eliot's translation is uneven, with fine moments:

Farmer: Good little fellow look to my horse,
I must go on foot through yonder gorse.
I'll find the rogue and give him one:
He'll rue as far as he can run.   (p. 368)

---

[16]See E. Catholy, *Fastnachtspiel* (Sammlung Metzler, 56), Stuttgart, 1966, pp. 18-20, and M. Beare, *Hans Sachs Selections*, University of Durham, 1983, p. lxxxviii ff.

and elsewhere with less felicitous efforts, as he struggles, and ultimately fails, to do justice to Sachs - for example, in the passage immediately preceding the above:

Farmer (offhand):
        How now little fellow?

Student (stupidly):
        Luck?

Farmer: Good luck!
        Hast thou seen one hereabouts run full tilt
        With back bowed under a pack of guilt?

Student (vaguely):
        Ya - just now - over yonder - ran
(very graphically though stupidly)
        Puff, pant, sweat, snort! - like under a ban!

On occasion, Eliot seems to go as far as giving up the unequal struggle, and edits the text to a more manageable shape: the crucial last speech of the farmer is reduced from the original eighteen lines to a mere eleven. Additions and subtractions detract from any attempt, let alone Eliot's, to render Sachs faithfully.

Atkins's translation of *Der pawr im fegfewer*, which he terms variously a 'Shrovetide play' and a 'carnival play', was, like the present texts, prepared for a celebratory occasion - the Magnum Convivium of the Historical Society of King's College London, held on 27 October 1925. (The second drama *The Student in Purgatory*, apparently written by Atkins, is a 'nightmare in three scenes', a drama-à-clef concerning muddied oaf students facing a viva voce history examination.) Atkins reports that:

    having undertaken to furnish the Society with a translation, and
    being unable to discover one already in existence, I perforce turned
    translator myself, and found the task an excellent entertainment for

the spare hours of a Kentish holiday. [17]

A highly entertaining piece was the result: spirited, faithful to the form and content of the original, with few weaknesses: a translation which must have been fun for the actors to work with. Some of the real strengths are seen in the passage where the farmer starts to have some intimation that all is not well:

Farmer:	Odds boddikins, where can I be!
	This hole's so dark I cannot see
	[.............................]
	Hell and perdition where am I?
Ulrich:	You are in Purgatorium.
Farmer:	O tell me in plain English, come.
	No word of Latin do I know.
Ulrich:	Make ready for a dreadful blow.
	Alack, you are in purgatory.
Farmer:	O what a gruesome, dreadful story.
	But am I dead, then, tell me, pray?
Ulrich:	Oh yes, you've really passed away
	Your corpse has duly been interred.
Farmer:	This gets beyond a joke, my word!
	Am I then just my own poor soul?

(pp. 12-13)

There are many admirable features in Atkins's work: he keeps the language and the tone natural, with a flowing, humorous timbre, and there is barely a stilted moment. He seems to capture the spirit of the work, and in doing so does justice to Sachs's original.

By contrast, **Krumpelmann's** translation, *Brooding Calves,* is so stilted or stylised at times that the suspicion arises that it was made deliberately so for comic effect. This may be seen in three examples all taken from the same passage of the play (p. 438 f.):

---

[17]This was actually at Dymchurch, in August 1925.

Wife:	Put on the kraut and meat to stew And see that when the herdsman bloweth Our sow with our cow from the stable goeth. [............................]
Peasant:	Although my wife, as I've been thinking, With the calf to the butcher wished to hurry And cash it in for a great coat furry (!) [...................................]
Peasant:	[.......] from every worm a calfie My wife will then forget I'm daffy.

Given the utter idiocy of the peasant in this text, the play does lend itself to some extent to a stylised treatment: this translation, deliberately or otherwise, seems to specialise in groan-inducing, in a quasi-pantomime sense. This is certainly not a fair way to treat any Sachs play *as a whole*; but common to all translators, including the present translator, is the *occasional* use of wrenched rhyme and word dislocation, giving actors and audience alike a useful comic resource with which to play.

Ouless, in his *Seven Shrovetide Plays*, classifies his selection as either 'moralities' - such as the *Children of Eve, (Wie gott, der herr, Adam unnd Eva ihre kinder segnet, 1553),* and *Dame Truth (Fraw warheit mit dem paurn, 1550),* or 'farces' such as *The Wandering Scholar, (Der farent schueler ins paradeis, 1550),* and *The Horse Thief (Der roßdieb zw Fünsing, 1553).* He is at once the least faithful and the most scholarly translator of Sachs into English. He works from the Goetze edition of Sachs's *Sämmtliche Fastnachtspiele.* [18] Each play has a short general introduction and is furnished with brief prefatory notes. In his general introduction, Ouless praises Sachs's ironic humour and his 'shrewd understanding of the weaker side of human nature'. He goes on:

---

[18] *Hans Sachs. Sämmtliche Fastnachtspiele [...] in chronologischer Ordnung nach den Originalen,* ed. E. Goetze, 7 vols (Neudrucke deutscher Litteraturwerke 26, 27, 31, 32, 39, 40, 42, 43, 51, 52, 60, 61, 63, 64), Halle, 1880-87.

It would be hard to find a more matter-of-fact poet in the realm of literature. Of any feeling for romance, the deeper aspects of life, or for the beauty of nature, there is little trace; on the other hand, he has an unfailing eye for a dramatic situation or a picturesque scene, and these qualities combined with humour and high spirits make him excellent company. The moral of his story is always clearly defined, if we look for it in the right place. It is the petty vanities of mankind, the clumsy lies and unnecessary quarrels of ordinary, everyday people, that he holds up to scorn and ridicule; but like the wise dramatist he does not attempt to explain in a limited scope why the thorough-paced villains often get off scot-free. (pp. 6-7)

Writing about his own work, Ouless explains that a certain amount of cutting and transposing lines in the original proved necessary, with the introduction here and there of extra dialogue and stage directions. The principal alterations and insertions are noted in the introductions prefacing each play. He further adds that his is a very free version, making no claims to scholarship or to precision in translation, and his plays are intended for the actor, not the student. Although Ouless does make numerous changes, there is much to respect here: the evident affection for Sachs and a clear understanding of his strengths, gained from judging him by appropriate intellectual and dramatic yardsticks, the intention to make the plays playable above all, and the care with which extraneous elements are added - as opposed to certain other 'improvement schemes' outlined above.

With his *Wandering Scholar*, Ouless becomes the first to opt for a prose version since Chambers. Moreover, the play contains two borrowed songs: the wife's little song of joy from the original, 'Pauernmeidlein', is replaced with one taken from Nicholas Udall's *Roister Doister*: 'I mun be maried a Sunday' appears in Act 3 Scene iv. [19] The scholar, too, sings a snatch from a song, this time borrowed from *Gammer Gurton's Nedle*: 'I cannot eat but little meat' is taken from the song 'Back and syde go bare',

---

[19]The date of Udall's *Roister Doister* remains uncertain; it may be as early as 1552.

which appears in Act 2 Scene i. [20] Ouless's version also contains some extra characters: a number of neighbours are introduced, as is the figure of Hans Sachs himself, who at one point sits on stage working at a half-finished shoe and listening to the wife and the neighbours conducting a conversation wholly absent from the original. Stage directions are detailed and copious.

The effect of these changes is to make Ouless's version more of an adaptation than a translation, but the piece is not ineffective, particularly the ending, where the husband and wife are seen to be reconciled by Sachs himself, speaking for the occasion in verse and standing in a semi-circle of neighbours:

Hans Sachs: For peace at home and no discord
                I leave with you this final word.
                True love makes up what wisdom lacks;
                Weigh both, and see - so says Hans Sachs.

All: So says Hans Sachs.

(The farmer and his wife drink in turn then hand the tankard to the neighbours, who also drink. Curtain.   (p. 37)

The presence of a curtain tells us, more revealingly than any other new element, perhaps, that Ouless has taken Sachs well beyond the realm of the original *Fastnachtspiel.*

A brief survey of these older translations, all highly individual in character, reveals some valuable points. On the whole, verse is preferred to prose. Although the quality of the verse is variable and uneven within individual translations, it is arguable that verse translations of the plays will always be preferable to prose, in that verse represents the medium in

---

[20]*Gammer Gurton's Nedle* is thought to be by William Stevenson and to date from the early 1550s. Both this and *Roister Doister* can be found in *Four Tudor Comedies*, ed. W. Tydeman, Harmondsworth, Penguin, 1984.

which the original was couched. To opt for prose certainly brings advantages in terms of flexibility, and undoubtedly makes life far easier for the translator, but removing the formal discipline of verse makes a major change to the nature of the linguistic event the audience hears or reads, and inevitably to the shaping and delivery of thought.

On occasion, translators have been tempted to add highly descriptive stage directions where few or none at all were originally present; this seems undesirable, since it represents an attempt to enforce both a uniform presentation and a particular interpretation of the text. Where stage directions have been added to clarify matters for actors, or the reader, this arguably represents a lack of faith on the translator's part in the actor's or reader's ability to use his or her native wit, imagination, and innate understanding of humanity; or it is a symptom of modern desire, fuelled by custom, to have a definitive text to work from both in the theatre and in the lecture theatre.

This question of superfluous stage directions is not to be confused with that of general textual authenticity. Bastian reminds us of an important consideration when examining *Fastnachtspiele*, citing Merkel's view of this textual authenticity question:

> Ungewiß muß bleiben, inwiefern und in welchem Umfang die Spieltexte mit Blick auf die wechselnden Aufführungsbedingungen (örtliche Verhältnisse, Zusammensetzung des Spielerensembles, spezielle Erwartungen des Publikums) geändert worden sind. Die handschriftlich überlieferten Fastnachtspiele sind als blosse Grundlage für eine konkrete Aufführung oder als deren textlichen Wiedergabe zu verstehen, geben .... im grossen und ganzen die Dialoge so wieder 'wie sie einmal aufgeführt wurden' und stellen 'die ungefährliche schriftliche Fixierung einer gebräuchlichen Textvariante dar'. [21]

---

[21] Hagen Bastian, *Mummenschanz: Sinneslust und Gefühlsbeherrschung im Fastnachtspiel des 15. Jahrhunderts*, Frankfurt, 1983. Here (pp. 12-13) it is claimed that we cannot be certain to what extent the texts were changed with a view to differing conditions of performance: local conditions, who was in the ensemble, particular audience expectations.

Yet however much texts may vary, the presence of stage directions only in limited numbers is a characteristic feature of Sachs's carnival comedies; to add more, for whatever reason, is to add an undesirable and indeed otiose dimension.

Be that as it may, in the light of Bastian's caveat concerning textual authenticity, it would be folly for any translation of Sachs's carnival comedies, no matter how faithful it attempts to be to the original, to claim to be definitive. In the testing ground of live performance, any version is likely to be improved by the kind of variations which sixteenth-century performers would have made to Sachs's texts. Since translating, moreover, is an exercise involving innumerable variables, the present translations can only hope to represent *one* response, among many possible responses, to the particular challenge of rendering Sachs into English. [22]

As indicated in the *Introduction*, the present volume results from an attempt to make Sachs accessible to a wider audience, both for reading and acting. As we have seen, others have trodden the same path with varying degrees of success. It is hoped that the nature of the works presented here, together with the breadth of the selection, represents a qualitative advance over previous offerings and will invite wider interest in Sachs's carnival comedies.

The *Fastnachtspiel* manuscripts we still have must be taken as representing the basis for a particular performance, or the recording of a performance; generally they reproduce dialogue 'as it was played', and present to us 'an approximate written statement of a known and used textual variant'.

[22]Inexplicably, the translation of *Der doctor mit der grosen nasen* originally performed at Goldsmiths' College had one line missing. To make good the deficiency, the last 40 lines of the present translation were re-written over a year after that first performance, and, in parts, bear only a passing resemblance to the first version - both versions, though, having satisfied the translator. This proved a benign problem, but indicates just how imprecise a science translating can be.

2. Language and voice

One of the major challenges in translating Sachs's carnival comedies is to find the appropriate combination of linguistic register, tone, and style in English to recreate the flavour of the original. The translator is called upon to render a particular form of German used in a particular context into an English which will capture the essence of what is meant and deliver it in an appropriate manner.

It would be a churlish translator who did not find Sachs a pleasure to work on and work with. The Keller and Goetze edition used here, based on the *Nürnberger Folioausgabe*, shows us that Sachs's German is palpably modern - or rather, clearly no longer medieval - and readily accessible to the late twentieth-century reader of German, for all the apparent idiosyncrasies of its spelling and the antiquity or quaintness of some of its vocabulary and idioms. In this, Sachs's German is perhaps no more troublesome than other vernaculars of the epoch. Although it was not until the mid-to-late seventeenth century that written German started to become widely standardised, Sachs produced his works, as Könnecker reminds us, in the kind of German widely accepted in official and legal circles in southern German-speaking regions in the sixteenth century. [23] Sachs's plays, then, have a regional voice, based on the author's own Nuremberg usage. Significantly, we are dealing with a regional rather than a local voice: the latter might have been less accessible than that of Sachs.

Agreement seems to exist among critics that throughout Sachs's dramas there is a discernible 'flattening' of the linguistic register towards the range commanded by the reasonably educated middle rank of people: the author reflecting his own usage. Adam and Eve, God and Satan in his tragedies and comedies are seen to speak in roughly the same way as the peasants and the townsfolk of the carnival comedies. If this alleged

---

[23]B. Könnecker, *Hans Sachs*, Stuttgart 1971, (Sammlung Metzler, 94). Here, p. 19.

flattening were indeed a true feature of Sachs's language as a whole, it might seem to simplify things for the translator. Critics have, however, oversimplified the true state of affairs, for whilst this 'flattening', or meeting on the middle ground, is undeniably one feature of the language of the *Fastnachtspiele*, Sachs is far from monotonous. Könnecker does attempt to defend him against the rather sweeping generalisation that essentially he commanded only one mode of utterance, but she does so by saying that it was not untypical for a sixteenth-century writer to have neither an individual voice nor a generally accepted 'artistic' medium of expression. [24] Her defence, which essentially admits the 'charge' in its entirety, fails, however, to do justice to Sachs's ability, within an admittedly limited linguistic range, to make what seem dramatically vital and sometimes rather subtle differentiations between characters not necessarily of different rank, as we shall see.

We have, of course, few if any authentic yardsticks against which we can measure whether Sachs faithfully captures the presumably ruder and harsher notes of the southern German peasants' speech: peasants did not and never have generated literature as such, and any image we have of them, any echo we have of the peasant voice across the centuries, is inevitably gleaned through the eyes and ears of an educated writer. The equally educated modern critical reader or member of an audience is likely to have assembled a composite image of peasantry based far more on secondary sources than actual experience, and which is a historical rather than a contemporary image. If one seeks to authenticate Sachs's efforts by cross-references to other literary images of the peasantry in other cultures - for example in England *Gammer Gurton's Nedle* or the *Second Shepherds' Play* from the Wakefield Cycle - an unhelpful circularity of argument emerges. Here, peasants are portrayed as dull-witted, oafish, greedy, and

---

[24]B. Könnecker, *Hans Sachs*, p. 19.

unclean. From other sources one is told that peasants are easily duped by sophisticated townsfolk; but the popular saying that to find a fool in the country you must take one with you offers a salutary antidote to modern town- or city-based arrogance. Peasants may, then, be portrayed as sly as an Aesop fox, or as honest sons of toil, or they may be endowed with a rustically romantic nobility: it rather depends on the socio-political intent of the particular author. Ultimately, the modern reader is largely left to rely on his or her own prejudices when gauging whether Sachs portrays the peasantry with accuracy: but of course, these prejudices will, at least in part, have been informed by writers such as Sachs, and circularity cannot, it seems, be avoided.

Sachs does indeed avail himself of most of the commonly attributed characteristics when portraying his various peasants; and he seems, as far as may reasonably be judged, to have them speak in a suitable manner. But within certain limits he does produce variations, linguistic subtleties and finesses, which help both towards characterisation of individuals and the production of comic effect. The point is perhaps most clearly made in *The Farmer Carrying a Foal*, in the exchanges between Cuntz, the farmer, and Heintz, his peasant lad:

Heintz: The Jewish doctor sees your piss
           And straight away cries 'What is this?'
           And swears an oath you're up the pole!
           You're carrying a baby foal!

Farmer, seizing his belly:
           What was it that I just said?
           Misfortune's heaped upon my head.
           Am I to give birth to a horse?
           This pregnancy can't run its course (lines 247-54)

Here, for all his distress, Cuntz operates in terms of linguistic content and structure on a more sophisticated level than Heintz, who, though endowed with a certain crude relish for language, as can be seen from his earlier near music-hall routine with Isaac, and from the odd moment in the following, taken from the same play, is a linguistically, and indeed generally, cruder beast:

Heintz:	He squats down comfy as you please
	This morning, out beside the fence,
	And lays a whopper - frankincense
	It clearly weren't! And full of gristle! (lines 194-97)

The English version used in these two examples does little or nothing to embellish the original German, which is far from presenting the kind of dreary, featureless plain some critics would have us believe was Sachs's natural linguistic home. The language is vibrant, differentiated, and is clearly not some kind of middle-of-the-road compromise mode of expression.

In the context of this survey of Sachs's language and of the modes of expression he employs, the tone of the nobility and of the upper rank of people in Sachs's carnival comedies also deserves some attention. Their language - that of the educated - is readily available to the critic, and the authenticity of Sachs's reproduction may be far more easily judged than is the case when his peasants speak. It is here, perhaps, that the flattening tendency becomes more obvious, perhaps because language at the more sophisticated levels of society has always been, and still is, more liable to fluctuations of style and tone and texture than at the more common-or-garden level at which Sachs mainly trades: one need only think of the influence exerted over the development of the German language and over social manners by a modish and even slavish usage of French by educated Germans in the early years of the seventeenth century.

In *Dionisius the Tyrant*, the mighty Dionisius is barely distinguishable from his servants; in *The Inquisitor and all his Soup Cauldrons*, the Inquisitor, once his rhetoric and bombast fall away, is much like his Sexton; Paulina and the procuress talk a common language on equal terms in *The*

Crying Pup. There is a clear converging of tone and register used by the characters. This phenomenon does, of course, have a simple explanation: in all three of these dramas, Sachs is demonstrating that the rich, the powerful, and the exceptional figures in society, are just as human, just as fallible and vulnerable, as those surrounding them. Dionisius shares this very insight with Damon; the Inquisitor has it rammed down his throat; Paulina is duped because of her sympathy for, and indeed her identification with the procuress's supposed daughter. If characters of apparently differing ranks and stations in life speak in tones which merge, it can be no surprise: Sachs is using language here to make a specific point about the ultimate equality of people.

At times, then, Sachs does linguistically temper the utterances of his grander figures, as, at times, he elevates his baser material so that they meet on common ground: somewhere, of course, near to the language he himself uses. But just as he is capable of differentiating in modes of utterance between peasants, as we saw from the example of *The Farmer Carrying a Foal*, he also demonstrates his good ear for gradations of language among those of higher birth or with better education. On the evidence of *The Doctor with the Big Nose*, this faculty manifests itself particularly in his demonstration of the nuances of how language is used to express social and intellectual status. Shifts in linguistic register as part of verbal jousting form a valuable part of both the comic action and the social criticism in this play, as we shall see in the relevant chapter.

The features of the language and voice of Sachs's carnival comedies - sheer historical distance, use of dialect, a supposed flattening of register concealing subtle gradations, difficulty in identifying an authentic voice, particularly for the peasants but also to a certain extent for the educated - present the would-be translator with a number of problems and opportunities. The first decision for the translator must be whether to opt for modern English or some putative English equivalent of Sachs's sixteenth-century German. Given that one of the chief purposes of this edition is to make Sachs accessible to a wider audience, that decision was easily made. It is one thing to ask an audience to come to terms with authentic early English, of the sort found, for example, in *Gammer Gurton's Nedle*:

Enter Hodge from the fields:
> See so cham arayed with dablynge in the durt -
> She that set me to ditchinge ich wold she had the squrt!
> Was never poore soule that such a life had?
> Gog's bones, thys vylthy glaye hase drest me to bad!
>   (Act 1, Scene ii, lines 45-49)

but quite another to subject an audience to a combination of fake historicity and inescapable tweeness in an attempt to recreate something of the correct historical feel for a translation of Sachs: Leighton's use of 'thee' and 'thou' and other 'period' touches, (see above), whilst understandable, strikes just such a false note.

However, opting for modern English, natural enough in the circumstances, does bring with it certain problems. For one, English no longer possesses credible dialect resources, let alone the range of genuine dialects which still underpin modern 'high' German. Whilst regional accents, strongly marked in some cases, do exist in English, residual dialect words or forms tend to be regarded as quaint relics by the majority who do not command them, and are worn at times with inordinate pride by the minority who do. Historically, Bristol might once have been a good choice for a dialect into which to render Sachs, or perhaps Lincoln, but such speculation is redundant. The dialect dimension present in Sachs cannot legitimately be reproduced in modern English.

Finding the right voice for Sachs's characters tends, then, to be a matter of seeking the appropriate idiom and register rather than trying to find a regional dialect equating to that of Nuremberg. Faced with the need to reproduce some kind of regional flavour, combined with glimpses of country life, modern English writers and actors frequently resort to some kind of 'Mummerset' delivery of the *'Oi be glaaad they sheep baint lorst, oo ar'* school of coarse acting: an at times unfortunately patronising tone, deemed, it would seem, intrinsically comical. The present translator has tried to avoid the fake bucolic as far as possible in the written text, but recognises the easy and effective comic possibilities of delivering many of Sachs's lines in a pastiche regional country voice: in the original *Vita Brevis* production of *The Doctor with the Big Nose* at Goldsmiths' College, Wally performed throughout in a broad Norfolk accent to good comic effect, contrasting nicely with the more standard English pronunciation of the Doctor and the standard-but-occasionally-slipping English of the harassed Squire.

Another problem associated with opting for modern English - albeit of the luxurious sort - is that the translator may be sorely tempted to 'improve' on the original by rendering more subtly and to greater effect than in the original the characterising features of individuals' utterances, or the broad 'class'-identifying features of their language as a whole. It is to be hoped that the present translations have not strayed too far in that direction, though the resources of English in certain contexts, particularly in expressing the social tensions and the snobbery and one-upmanship in *The Doctor with the Big Nose*, for example, with its barely-expressed condescensions and pretensions, offer richer possibilities than are present in the original German.

One feature inherent in Sachs's carnival comedies does make the task of rendering them into modern English far easier than it might otherwise have been: there seems to be a timeless quality about the language, or rather about the way Sachs's characters express themselves and the things they talk about. This is more than a matter of language: it has to do with a certain cast of mind present in Sachs's characters which seems somehow familiar. Schütte talks of the widespread agreement among critics that Sachs's characters are true-to-life and may easily be identified with, that they are accessible, and acceptably realistic. [25] With this it is hard to argue. Yet he warns against an over-personalised approach into which critics seem to be drawn, and warns equally against cosy assumptions about Sachs representing and indeed portraying the 'common man': he is, in fact identifying the sort of circularity of argument outlined above, in the passage dealing with Sachs's capturing of the right voice for his peasants. The way out of this problem is indicated by the approach of Müller, [26] who sees Sachs's characters not as individuals but as representative types who are used principally to illustrate variations on the theme of the seven deadly sins - and, one might add, the proverbial wisdoms which are distillations of the experiences gained in succumbing to sin or indeed warding off temptation to sin. [27]

It is small wonder that Sachs's creations seem familiar, seem to speak about the things which concern us all, and react to the trials of life in ways with which a modern audience can incline to identify: they are us, we are their heirs, and it is the common bonds of human weakness, the age-old reaction both to grand-scale temptations and to the small and irksome vicissitudes of daily life which link us and which make modern readers and theatregoers empathise so readily with what are only at best lightly-sketched characters, at worst the crudest of thumbnail sketches. This

---

[25] J. Schütte, 'Was ist unser freyhait nutz / wenn wir ir nicht brauchen durffen. Zur Interpretation der Prosadialoge', in *Hans Sachs - Studien zur frühbürgerlichen Literatur im 16. Jahrhundert*, ed. T. Cramer and E. Kartschoke, Bern, 1978. Here, p. 42 ff.

[26] Maria E. Müller, 'Bürgerliche Emanzipation und protestantische Ethik. Zu den gesellschaftlichen und literarischen Voraussetzungen von Sachs' reformatorischen Engagement', in T. Cramer and E. Kartschoke, *Hans Sachs,* pp. 11-40. See especially p. 30 ff.

[27] See R. E. Schade, *'Das Narren schneyden (1557).* The Deadly Sins and the Didactics of Hans Sachs', in *Studies in Early German Comedy 1500-1650*, Columbia, South Carolina, 1980, pp. 73-95.

is why Sachs travels so well through time - far better, dare one say, than some of his more illustrious colleagues from the canon of German literature, whose interests are more specific and localised in time and space.

With his carnival comedies, Sachs proved and proves equipped to survive in a wider market place because he talks in simple illustrative terms about quasi-eternal problems affecting the bulk of humanity in their everyday lives. Plots may vary - from the problems of the peasant to those of the inquisitor - but the subject under investigation is the very stuff of human frailty. These carnival plays remind their audience, at a time of greatest apparent licence and greatest temptation to err, of their mortal weaknesses and of the human and social consequences of abandoning both rectitude and the salutary wisdoms familiar from the realm of proverbs. To find a voice in translation for these characters and for these issues, is, in part, to voice one's own understanding of the lower common denominators of human behaviour.

3. Form

Formal considerations can at times prove irksome for the modern mind, accustomed in the latter half of the twentieth century to drama being largely in prose, and to poetry largely setting aside the stricter forms of earlier centuries. Matching the regular rhyme scheme of Sachs's verse - rhyming couplets - together with the relentless stride of the four-stress line, does not in itself present any problem to the translator. There is, however, a curious effect when using this sort of form in English: it is perhaps something inherent in the language itself, or a matter of the twentieth-century English ear being all too familiar with the patterns of comic expectation aroused when a limerick looms into view. There seems to exist a certain predisposition towards the comic, not infrequently of the ribald sort, when English takes to the rhyming couplet, and in particular when the feminine ending is subtly wielded. An English audience might, then, find itself encouraged to find Sachs amusing simply because the retained form of the original - which contrives by means of its insistent metre to hurry the listener towards an anticipated rhyme, thus setting up the possibility in every line, or at least every second line, of a comic twist - alerts them to certain possibilities.

As far as the discipline of retaining word order is concerned, on occasion it is all too easy to succumb to the temptation of using inversion to find the perfect rhyme, be it for enhanced comic effect or simply to render accurately the original - and of this the present translator is as guilty as his predecessors, although it was his policy to try to make word-order as natural as possible throughout.

Finding an appropriate way of rendering Sachs's rhythm and stress patterns presents a more serious set of problems. Sachs wrote many of the plays in this selection some seventy years before Martin Opitz appeared on the scene to illuminate a literary-poetic world where German-language poetry (and poetic drama) was perceived to be 'disadvantaged' in comparison to that of neighbouring countries such as France, England, Italy, and Holland. That two of the key propositions made by Opitz in his *Buch von der deutschen Poeterey* (1624) were to have the natural stress of the word coincide with the chosen metrical pattern of the poem, and to have German writers, for the time being, stick closely to using iambic and trochaic feet, venturing only rarely to use the more exotic dactyl, comes as a mild shock. With the exception of certain works produced by pioneering Germans largely living abroad, who were abreast of the latest literary developments outside the German-speaking territories, poetry produced in German at the beginning of the seventeenth century was still clinging to the syllable-counting tradition of the Meistersinger, where natural emphases were sacrificed to the dominance of an overarching metrical pattern. Opitz's recommendations might be deemed, in a different context, rather to resemble a beginners' 'follow the magic footsteps' guide to the waltz or the foxtrot; to the modern mind, and no doubt to Shakespeare and his contemporaries had they read it, the verse of Sachs and his ilk might at times resemble a demonstration of a somewhat a-rhythmic clog dance. But let us not fall into the trap of comparing like with unlike: as Leighton reminds us, Sachs's Pegasus never soared over the loftiest heights of Olympus, and did not wish to do so. Nor, one might add, would it have been capable of doing so, even given the historical opportunity. Sachs's poetry, like his dramatic verse, has to be judged by the appropriate standards. Any translation of Sachs's carnival comedies into modern English will have at its disposal, and almost inevitably have recourse to, rhythms and stress patterns beyond the range of the originals. Again, the authenticity of any such translation might be seen to be a problem, but as with the question of dialect resources on the one hand, or linguistic subtleties on the other, it must be accepted that there can be no perfect match between sixteenth-century German and twentieth-century English, and to look for such a match is wrong-headed.

Critic and translator alike should not be irked by the fact that with Sachs they are not dealing with Goethe or Shakespeare: Sachs is a middle-brow writer bound by what now seem the archaic and even stultifying formal literary conventions of his age, conventions which were to need radical reappraisal in the next century. To kick against the reality of Sachs's work in this respect is rather like complaining that a squash player, bound to and by the formal conventions of that game, is not playing lawn tennis, or that a merry-go-round horse, fixed to its pole and its repetitive cycle, is not a steeplechaser jumping fences.

The translator of Sachs's carnival comedies is faced with an ineluctable need to make the translation differ from the original in a number of ways, one of which is clearly this realm of stress patterns and rhythm. Modern English cannot be forced back into the syllable-counting, emphasis-wrenching mode of sixteenth-century Germany, but must be allowed its natural freedoms: by enjoying those freedoms and emancipating itself from certain formal constraints present in the original it can do fullest justice to the spirit of Sachs's plays. It is hoped that the translations which follows here do precisely that: capture the spirit of Sachs's works, and render his carnival comedies into a form where more people can come to appreciate their undoubted excellence.

4. CARNIVAL, PLAYS, AND PLAYING

The subject of carnival activities has recently aroused considerable attention. We may glean a great deal from social historians concerning the significance of carnival in the broader context of early modern Germany - an activity seen at the extremes of interpretation as a covert method for exercising social control whilst pretending to encourage license, or as an innocent once-a-year celebration which also acted as a safety valve, enabling a release of energy and encouraging the using up of soon-to-be-forbidden comestibles before the imposed rigours of Lent. [1] Whatever one's interpretation of the forces in play, **playing** itself formed an essential feature of sixteenth-century German Shrovetide and other carnival activities. Aside from the normal social pursuits and games - card-playing, drinking, dancing, amorous dalliances, bear-baiting, or any combination of these and other amusements, depending upon tastes - this playing often took the form of role-playing by individuals, seen in its simplest

---

[1]Useful recent contributions to an understanding of the early modern period and its social and cultural history come from Bob Scribner, 'Reformation, carnival and the world turned upside down', in *Social History*, 3:iii, 1978, pp. 303-29, (also translated as 'Reformation, Karneval und die verkehrte Welt', in *Volkskultur*, ed. R. van Dülmen and N. Schindler, Frankfurt, 1984, pp. 117-52; R. Po-Chia Hsia (ed.), *The German People and the Reformation*, Ithaca, 1988; and M. Hughes, *Early Modern Germany,* London, 1992.

manifestation in fancy-dress events, and often extended to embrace an individual playing at being king or queen for a day. [2] Playing, though, also assumed the more co-ordinated form of a dramatic presentation.

Clearly Sachs's role was as a provider of the latter kind of activity. It should be remembered, however, that all of these various pursuits, these individual ways of playing, formed but part of a wider pattern. Events which together made up a carnival celebration inevitably competed for attention. In their original calendar position and performed in public places rather than private houses, Sachs's carnival comedies and their players, like fire-eaters or fortune-tellers, jugglers or sellers of magic potions, were literally in a market for the attention of the general public. The attention span of an assembled public being inevitably short at the best of times, and in all likelihood considerably shortened by a carnival atmosphere, the dramas had, of necessity, to be brief and bright, capable of grabbing the attention and holding it. The seizing of the moment was accomplished in a number of ways in Sachs's carnival comedies, but principally by the introductory lines to the individual dramas, which tended to be in the form of an announcement contained within the action but directed simultaneously towards arousing the curiosity of the audience, [3] or an attention-grabbing statement of the perhaps alarmingly familiar sort, given the environment, [4] or a direct address to the audience, inviting their complicity with the characters. [5] Once gained, attention was retained by

---

[2]This indeed forms the core of the action in *Dionisius the Tyrant*.

[3]See the opening lines of *The Doctor with the Big Nose*:
'Good news I hear from far away
My dearest friend arrives today!'

[4] See the opening lines of *The Farmer Carrying a Foal*:
'Oh wife, my belly's in a state -
And yet I wasn't drinking late.'

[5]See the opening lines of *The Red-hot Poker*:
'Our marriage is just four years old
And my husband's love grown all but cold.'

the sheer pace of the dramas, the lack of distraction in the form of scene changes and props, and the simple, amusingly-portrayed home truths being enacted for the audience. [6]

We know, of course, that Sachs's plays are and were performed over a longer 'season' than the days immediately preceding Lent, and that they were also performed in private houses, but their nature was dictated to no inconsiderable extent by the demands of fitness for purpose imposed by carnival as a many-faceted, public celebratory event.

The carnival activities and seasonal events of which Sachs's carnival comedies formed a part are themselves not infrequently reflected in the plays, and occasional cross-referencing helps explain to the modern reader more about sixteenth-century carnival pursuits. One small example of this is the apparently cryptic reference to 'fetching the bacon in the Deutscher Hof', which makes a brief appearance in *Evil Fumes*. [7] The context for the reference, and its significance, are explained in another play - *Ein schoen kurtzweilig faßnachtspiel mit dreyen personen, nemlich ein kelner und zwen bawren, die holen den bachen im teutschen hoff* [8] (*A Merry Shrovetide Play with Three Players: a Cellarer and two Peasants, who bring home the Bacon from the Teutscher Hof*) - where it transpires that fetching the bacon home was a traditional virility test: the husband who can prove with the aid of

---

or the opening lines from *Evil Fumes*:
'I bid you welcome goodly Sirs
And ask of you to lend your ears
To my complaint about my wife.'

[6]For discussions of the staging and presentation of Sachs's carnival comedies see H. Krause, *Die Dramen des Hans Sachs. Untersuchungen zur Lehre und Technik*, Berlin, 1979, p. 113 ff.; E. Catholy, *Fastnachtspiel*, pp. 18-20; and K. Wedler, *Hans Sachs*, Leipzig, 1976, p. 109 ff.

[7]*Evil Fumes*, lines 40-42. The original reads:
'Des ich seidt-her hab dieser sachen
Im deutschen hof den schweinen pachen
nie holen dörffen, auff mein eid.'

[8]Keller and Goetze, Vol. 5, p. 31 ff.

testimony from a number of witnesses that he is lord and master of his house (or better yet get his wife so to testify) can take home the side of smoked bacon hanging up in the local tavern. It has, of course, been hanging there for a very long time. [9]

Another Shrovetide custom, which saw neighbours slaughter and cure their pigs and offer each other gifts of sausage, forms the subject of *Der gestolen pachen (The Stolen Bacon),* where Heintz Knol and Cuntz Drol decide to steal a side of salted bacon from their avaricious neighbour, Herman Dol. [10] He, in turn, plans to excuse himself from giving gifts to his neighbours by saying he does not understand the custom, thus enabling him to make his sausages last further into the period of fasting to come. That the local cleric helps Heintz and Cuntz in their nefarious purpose is not insignificant: avarice and lack of charity are rudely punished.

Whilst these plays contain instructive details concerning Shrovetide customs and practices, it is outside the context of the carnival comedies altogether where Sachs gives the clearest idea of his conception of Shrovetide and its attendant celebrations. In his *Historia: Das fest der abgöttin Bona Dea (A True History: the Festival of the Goddess Bona Dea),* [11] Sachs talks of pagan rites attached to a sylvan deity in Roman times. The story told is taken from Plutarch, and concerns a frustrated attempt to commit adultery through the use of disguise. A young man, Clodius, tries to infiltrate a strictly women's festival in order to make love to Pompeia, the wife of Julius Caesar. Discovered, he is summoned before the authorities the next day but released unpunished as a result of pressure from the people: 'der gemeine mann'. Caesar, however, punishes his wife

---

[9]The equivalent tradition in England is that of the *Dunmow Flitch,* which goes back at least as far as 1445. To win the side of bacon in question, the husband has to testify that during the past year and a day he has not repented of his marriage.

[10]Keller and Goetze, Vol. 14, pp. 220-32.

[11]Keller and Goetze, Vol. 20, pp. 368-72.

for merely being implicated in a potentially scandalous situation. Sachs concludes that this sort of festival spawned 'modern' Shrovetide celebrations, being:

> gwislich ursprung und anfang
> Auch unser faßnacht-mummerey,
> Da man sich verkleidt mancherley,
> Die männer offt in frawenkleider,
> Und in mannsgewand die frawen leider

(certainly the origins of our carnival masquerades, when people frequently dress up, the men often in womens' clothing, the women, regrettably, in men's clothing) [12]

Sachs goes on to warn that the fun and games, the playing and dancing, which form an integral part of carnival, provide the ideal opportunity for immoral, irregular, and socially disruptive behaviour. Fortunately, he says, God's word drove out such heathen rites, and God should be obeyed today, even in the context of carnival:

> Gott wöll, daß sein wort reichlich wachs
> Und vil frucht bring, das wünscht Hans Sachs.
> (13th May, 1563)

(God desires his word to spread vigorously and to bring forth fruit, which is also the wish of Hans Sachs.)

These thoughts from the mature Sachs provide a key to understanding what his attitude to the potential licentiousness of carnival was, and they reflect some of the vital features of carnival: the use of disguise to cross social barriers, a tendency towards relative moral laxness or even turpitude, and, despite or because of the latter, depending on one's point of view, the containment of the rites and rituals within the broad and unchanging Christian framework.

---

[12]The donning of the man's trousers by the woman, having won them in domestic 'battle', is the subject of *Evil Fumes*.

Another, complementary, view of carnival is revealed in Sachs's *Ein gesprech mit der Faßnacht von ihrer aygenschafft*, of 18 February 1540 (*A Conversation with Shrovetide Concerning its Nature*). [13] In this allegorical piece, Sachs is walking on the Friday after the Shrovetide celebrations by the river Pegnitz in Nürnberg, and peering into a now empty purse. He takes fright at the sight of a huge, fantastic creature, covered in bells, with a belly like a barrel, great teeth, a vast maw, a shorn tail, no ears or eyes, and a human voice. The creature introduces itself as 'Faßnacht', the personification of carnival, and outlines all it has eaten and drunk, and responds to questioning about its bells with a list of the fun and games people get up to during carnival - including singing and dancing, gambling, fireworks, games of strength and skill, and, significantly, dressing up in disguise:

> Viel fassnacht-spiel bring ich herbey
> Und an zal gar viel mummerey
> Die sich vermummen und verbutzen
> Ein thails wie weyber sich auff-mutzen
> Eins thails wie münch, eins teils wie morn.
> Wer sich der nerrischst stellen kann
> Der ist der best und hat den preiss
> Von wegen nerrischer abweis.

> (I am the bringer of many carnival games and masquerades; some dress as women, some as monks, some as moors; the maddest disguise gets the prize.)

The creature has huge teeth and a cavernous maw to enable it to consume at a vast rate people's clothes, money, furniture, household goods, houses, fields, and sundry property. Such losses lead them into irrecoverable debt and poverty, sinfulness and disgrace - via a path of cheating, whoring, and adultery - and condemn them to a life of miserable drudgery and disease.

---

[13]Keller and Goetze, Vol. 5, pp. 295-99.

The creature has neither eyes nor ears, since the identity of those it attacks remains a matter of complete indifference, and thus it has no need to know who they are, nor does it listen to pleas for mercy or to imprecations from the pious. The creature wreaks personal and social havoc for two or three months at a time, then, exhausted, departs to recover in time for the coming year. Sachs concludes with a well-meant warning: that everyone, and this is conceived of as the masculine 'er', should enjoy carnival celebrations in moderation so as to avoid wasting their precious resources on one binge, for which they, plus their wives and children, will have to pay dearly all the rest of the year. [14]

This work is revealing on two accounts: firstly, in its assumption that society is male-dominated and that Shrovetide is a particularly male celebration, bringing with it the real possibility that men will neglect their family responsibilities; second, in its concentration on material considerations, indeed its complete neglect of a religious, ethical, or in any way spiritual dimension. On the first point: it has been clearly pointed out by Scribner [15] that shrovetide carnival activities were focused on young, *single* men; indeed the Reformation itself found its most fertile reception among young and upwardly-striving men. In the world-turned-upside-down mood of carnival, this section of society found expression for their ambitions, and could give vent to their frustrations. The new and young sought, in play at least, to oust the old and apparently immobile, using satire and parody, or travesty, to impress upon others their sense of frustrated ambition, and their criticisms of the stable, conservative, hierarchical society in which they lived. Sachs's appeal to *married* men not to neglect their family role should not lead us to modify any assumptions about the nature of carnival, but rather to recognise that carnival was and

[14] For further discussion of Sachs's attitude to Fastnacht see M. E. Müller, *Der Poet der Moralität. Untersuchungen zu Hans Sachs*, Bern, 1985.

[15] See Van Dülmen and Schindler, *Volkskultur*, p. 133.

is indeed difficult for anyone to resist. Even if unattached young men are its principal movers, married men risk jeopardising domestic stability by succumbing to the temptation of the many self-indulgent excesses offered during the carnival period. They have most to lose when enjoying the temporary licence of Shrovetide celebrations. Sachs's evident desire to ensure that marriages remain secure and that domestic circumstances do not deteriorate as a result of licentious and irresponsible behaviour - a desire reflected in a number of the plays in this selection - leads us to the second point: that of Sachs's concern being for the material rather than spiritual damage which carnival can cause, and for promoting sensible moderation and the common good. [16]

Given the Lutheran doctrine of the priesthood of all believers, and the possibility of salvation lying solely in the quality of the individual's faith, it is hardly surprising that Sachs does not refer in this work to ecclesiastical restrictions or the need to justify one's actions to a priest, particularly a Catholic priest. Müller argues that Sachs's reception of Luther's doctrine was selective, and tailored to be applicable to his own circumstances as a property-owning master cobbler - not exactly the representative of the 'common man', given his economic status, but, though an upright trader and craftsman, certainly not more than the rough equivalent of lower-middle class in modern terms. [17] For Sachs, the prosperity of the community was uppermost: stability and economic security remained uppermost in his mind, reinforced by a desire to have the community avoid at least the seven deadly sins, particularly sloth or idleness, known to lead to criminal behaviour and in itself both unproductive and a sign of socio-economic problems. Luther's theology and social vision is interpreted into

---

[16]For further discussions of Sachs's values see A.-K. Brandt, *Die 'tugentreich fraw Armut'. Besitz und Armut in der Tugendlehre des Hans Sachs (Gratia, 4)*, Göttingen, 1979; and also H. Krause, *Die Dramen des Hans Sachs*, pp. 47-88.

[17]See M. E. Müller, 'Bürgerliche Emanzipation', in T. Cramer and E. Kartschoke, *Hans Sachs*, p. 13 ff.

simple practical terms both by Sachs and, indeed, by the city fathers of Nuremberg; the Lutheran freedom of a Christian man is not to be confused with absolute licence, even during carnival.

Sachs's carnival comedies reflect his concern to control the dangerous and anti-social forces inherent in carnival activities *from the inside*. Very few of these plays, designed for performance amid the hurly-burly of carnival, and often focusing on the potential breakdown of marital relationships or some other threat to order and stability, will allow the audience to escape without being given a clear moral directive, a firm antidote to the unstable and potentially destabilising situation depicted. Of those in this selection, only *The Crying Pup* is overtly negative in tone, shocking the audience into a sense of outrage and injustice, and leading it to reaffirm its faith in love and marriage. The negative conclusion of *The Inquisitor with all his Soup Cauldrons* is, of course, of a different order, and is meant to form an indictment of the corrupt and decadent Catholic Church. Generally, though, Sachs's carnival comedies reflect the broader pattern of the events of which they form a part. They mirror the nature and function of carnival in allowing the threat of disorder, before reimposing sanity and stability, for the common good.

Der Falsche klaffer.

WElch mensch ist so vnbescheyden
Den leuten thůt je ehr abschneyden
Hinderruck auß neyd vnde haß
Mit lůg vnd list on vnterlaß
Steltman jm red der schmechwort sein
So leugt ers als wider hinein
Vnd macht darfür ein plaßen dunst
Das ist des klaffers list vnd kunst
Das gifftig maul kan niemandt fliehen
Wann er kan eim sein zungen ziehen
Mit schmeychel worten vnd heuchlerey
Sam er trew vnd verschwigen sey
Was man jm thůt auff trawen sagen
Das thůt er darnach weyter tragen
Vnd leuget allmal mer darzů
Das er die sach auffmuntzen thů
Nichts heimlichs bleybt bey jm verschwiger
Sein ach vnd krach ist schwatzen vnd liegen
Vnd die leut an einander hetzen
Das sie mit zanck einander wetzen
Denn zeucht er den kopff auß der schlingen
Redt auch das ergst zů allen dingen
Vnd forschet stets nach newen meeren
Verheysset vil vnd helt nit gern
Geet nur vmb mit verschrenckten worten
Vnd sucht auff flucht an allen orten
Thůt mit betrug sein gůter men
Mit falschem zůsagen vnd ayd schweren
Der auch die lewt kan wol vexieren
Mit spot vnd hönworten schumpffieren
Wenn man jm der gleich wil vergelten
So thůt er schmehen/schenden vnd schelten
Mit worten gifftig/heiß/vnd spitzig
Vnbescheyden in zoren hitzig
Wünscht Frantzosen vnd ander plag
Auch lestert er Got vber tag
Mit Sacrament/kyden/vnd todt
Also er menschen vnd auch Got
Belaidigt durch sein falsches maul
Dem solt man als eim bösen gaul
Ein schloß schlagen für sein zungen
Das er zů schweygn wurd gezwungen
Das wer sein wol verdienter lon
So blib mit friden yederman
Als dise Figur zayget an.

Gedruckt durch Hans Guldenmundt.
1 5 4 7.

1. *The Calumniator*, Georg Pencz, 1536.

5. THE DOCTOR WITH THE BIG NOSE

Ein faßnachtspil mit vier personen
Der doctor mit der grossen nasen
13 December 1559

Created specifically for performance, and adapted during the course
of staging, this English version of *The Doctor* evolved into perhaps the
freest of all the translations in this volume. It is also the only one where
German names have been changed to an English equivalent.

In using the subject matter of a famous diplomat scholar visiting the
local squire in the latter's somewhat pretentious country seat, and suffering
dreadful embarrassments at the hands of the squire's barely house-trained
servants, Sachs might be thought to be venturing a little out of the familiar
territory of carnival comedy. In broad terms, marital squabbles and
skulduggery among the (lower) urban classes, or scenes of mind-numbing
stupidity played out by oafish peasants, tend to form the staple fare for
carnival comedies, both by Sachs and others. But any notion that the
Fastnachtspiel as a genre, and Sachs as a major contributor to that genre,
cannot address issues from outside the common realm of daily low-level
existence deserves challenging. It is undoubtedly true that when he
ventures into the realm of tragedy Sachs does not scale the lofty
intellectual heights, nor create the linguistic subtlety and majesty those
schooled in the classical and neo-classical traditions have come to expect;

he manifestly falls short of creating figures of regal splendour and dignity, and indeed fails to create any impression of majesty and wonder. But it should not lightly be assumed that within the medium of carnival comedy he was incapable of portraying those of a higher rank accurately: indeed, the opposite is true. Sachs's strategy is that of portraying the very human weaknesses of the aristocracy and others of high rank, weaknesses which are subsumed under the general category of human folly and which are the very stuff of carnival drama. The selection of Sachs's carnival comedies presented in this volume has a range of characters from peasant to tyrant, from patrician wife to Papal inquisitor, from innkeeper to procuress, from merchant moneylender to quack doctor, from squire to fool. If, as has been pointed out above (pp. 15-20), these characters all seem to talk roughly the same language and all rub shoulders comfortably in Sachs's world, it is precisely because Sachs investigates their common heritage of all-too-human weakness rather than their distinctions of rank or birth or intellect.

Thus Sachs's purpose in this play is neither to pay homage to the alleged excellent qualities of the Doctor, nor to portray exquisite social and intellectual intercourse between the squire and his old friend, but to use the *faux naif* fool, Wally, to expose the wafer-thin veneer of the conventional behaviour, the very civilisation to which the two members of the upper rank pay lip service. The common currency of baser thoughts and instincts underlying the courtly pretentiousness of the Doctor and the squire make them no loftier mortals than the calculatingly odious Wally and the hapless Fred. Sachs brings our attention to bear, in an oddly Lutheran way, on the subject of equality, an equality expressed in the belief that we are all subject not only to the Fall, but to the pettinesses and irritating flaws either inherent in all mankind or implanted by social conditioning. This is not to say that Sachs is presenting us here with a socio-analytical treatise. His theme actually needs little explanation: the 'emperor's new clothes' syndrome is easily comprehended, the corruption of all mankind is so familiar to even the dullest of wits, that Sachs is on well-prepared territory in exposing such flaws, and can proceed apace, confident that his message will fall on readily receptive ears. Some might, of course, be embarrassed by the message; but in the context of most performances of carnival comedies, held in only a minority of cases in private houses, those of patrician or nobler rank would be clearly outnumbered by those predisposed to hear and enjoy criticism of their masters and betters.

The Doctor with the Big Nose hinges on an unplanned reunion of two old friends - or are they merely acquaintances? - which is ruined by the presence of the socially untrammelled fool, Wally. But before the anarchic interventions of the fool, Sachs carefully engineers a situation fraught with incalculable ingredients. The Doctor is described in superlatives by the Squire: is this all true, or is the Squire seeking to draw attention to his own status by citing an instance of the sort of friend he has: vicarious accreditation of his pedigree? The fact that he has to enjoin his servant, Fred, to treat the guest with proper deference and decorum implies a number of things: most revealingly, that Fred is not a properly trained servant used to dealing with noble visitors, which in turn indicates that the Squire either does not have such visitors, or has not previously deemed it necessary to train his servants, or has failed to train or have them trained properly. These possibilities lead to speculation about the Squire's status and his authority. Fred, of course, is but a groom ('Reitknecht'), as we discover in the *dramatis personae*. The reader - less so the audience, who have subtler clues to work on, such as Fred's interpretation of his master's orders being largely confined to grooming the horse and polishing the Doctor's boots - suspects that this 'court' might indeed be one where staff are thin on the ground and difficult to distinguish from their master. The comparison with the 'real' court of Dionisius, as portrayed in *Dionisius the Tyrant*, is instructive. A certain tense expectation is engendered: what will the worldly diplomat make of this makeshift court? Fred it is who introduces the next element of tension: the presence of the unpredictable fool. Summoned, Wally gives a virtuoso first speech: his values are wholly earthly, his respect and allegiance owed to the best provider of food and drink, his culinary evocations aimed directly at the saliva glands and gastric juices of the Shrovetide audience. There is little time for the Squire to chide him, as the Doctor is seen to be approaching, but just enough for Sachs to reveal yet more uncertainty: the Squire has not seen the Doctor - now a famous scholar and courtier - for some ten years. Sachs, then, builds in the possibility of the loss of any real contact which might once have existed between the two, and of their paths, if they ever were close, having diverged massively, which is indeed the case. The greeting from the Squire is warm to the point of effusiveness. The Doctor can only respond with a mildly embarrassed rebuff: he cannot stay long, he has only dropped in on his way to an appointment in Bamberg. And here the social games commence, as mutual sounding out combines with jostling for position and establishing of superiority.

The Squire's first gambit is to have his servant Frederick (where did Fred disappear?) serve not standard German white, but *red* wine. Its chief characteristic for the Squire is its strength ('ein starcken drunck' - 'a good red wine with a bit of bite'), and it rapidly disappears down his throat. The Doctor, not as quick off the mark, offers a retrospective toast for which the Squire allowed no time, and which clearly did not cross the latter's mind. Relishing the prospect of the full-blooded wine, the Doctor indulges in the one-upmanship of the wine connoisseur, naming the possible source of the wine in question: he is perhaps the first wine bore in German literature. The actor portraying him, cursed of course with an outsize nose, can make much business of attempting to manoeuvre the glass to his lips, virtually inviting the intervention of Wally: indeed, the present translation invites Wally's intervention with the pun on the 'nose' of the wine. Even before

Wally starts on his disastrous course, Sachs has already done much, as we see, to establish the uneasy atmosphere, the tensions and cross-currents informing the action. Wally, temporarily displaying greater social niceties than his own master, toasts the Doctor before launching into the attack: the nose is characterised as a roosting perch for seven hens, the king of the noses, and a beautiful candle-snuffer. It is not, of course, the embarrassed Doctor who promptly loses control, but the Squire: his language descends several levels for four lines, then he attempts to restore order by inviting the Doctor to inspect his new country seat: not without a hint of vulgar, *nouveau riche* ostentation. The Doctor's response remains neutral in tone.

Having sidled back onto an empty stage, Wally can expand on the theme of the nose - quite revoltingly, with imagery calculated to delight and disgust the audience simultaneously - and plan the action for us: an early example of the use of distancing techniques, later to be integral to Brecht's conception of epic theatre. [1] Fred's role, from now on, will be reduced to that of intermittently hustling Wally offstage, with an increasing degree of violence, and acting as the 'straight man', the voice of reason, giving the counterpoise to Wally's increasingly reckless plans and actions. By the time the Doctor and the Squire return from looking at the architectural delights of the house, the audience can expect a reprise of Wally's nose speech - this time denying the reality of the situation, but drawing attention nonetheless to the Doctor's deformity. But Sachs has another plot running: the steadily deteriorating relationship between the Doctor and the Squire. Forced to admit the glories of the building, the Doctor attacks the Squire's vulnerable point, his library: that is, the books rather than the room, a library the Squire has no doubt improved in the last ten years, picking up at least some of the many good books made

---

[1]For an analysis of the relationship between Brecht's theatre and Fastnachtspiel, see T. Habel, *Brecht und das Fastnachtspiel. Studien zur nicht-aristotelischen Dramatik*, Göttingen, 1978.

available through the medium of the printing press. This is a wonderfully unsubtle intellectual insult, linked with an equally pointed financial slight. The Squire responds by putting both feet firmly in his mouth (Fred had earlier identified precisely this propensity in Wally in his first speech): he buys only German-language books, at a time when, for all Luther's efforts, Latin continued to predominate as the language for serious discourse, and indeed buys them *by the pile*. His pseudo-intellectual gloss about being an unlearned layman using books to expand his mind scarcely improves the situation. But before the two can see the treasury of books, Wally intervenes with more of what, from the audience's point of view, is splendidly ludicrous and humiliating imagery to describe the nose. The effect is that the Doctor voices something approaching regret that he came to visit at all. The violence of the Squire's response represents an escalation of his reaction to the first such incident, whilst his efforts to pour oil on troubled waters become all the more strained. Rattled, he invites the Doctor to see the library, but gives away more of his false pretensions to intellectuality with his list of what is to be seen, and particularly the order of that list: above all, since last of all on the list and capping the speech, a number of 'good yarns' ('guet schwenk'). The two leave with an implied threat from the Doctor hanging in the air - don't let this happen again! - together with more explicit and perhaps somewhat ungentlemanly descriptions of the violence the Squire would like to mete out to Wally.

Sachs now reprises the pattern of Wally's disingenuous wonderment, regret, and determination to recover the situation - by digging an even deeper hole for himself, as the audience can see - and combines it with Fred's warnings and admonishments. Wally has thus far drawn attention to the hugeness of the nose; he has pretended it is tiny; he will now go to great lengths to heal the situation by telling the Doctor he will not mention his nose again. All is set up for a final showdown. When the Doctor and the Squire return, the Doctor speaks only of the quantity of the Squire's books: again, the insult is subtle, but not to be missed; (the reference to 'piles' in the English version adds a dimension not in the original, but might make a useful comic resource for the actors). Wally, grossly over-familiar as usual, slaps the Doctor on the shoulder and says he will not mention the offending nose again. The contrast between this intervention and the lofty sentiments just uttered by the Doctor concerning the merits of a literary education is delightfully pointed. Now the Squire reaches a zenith of violent reaction, graphically outlining the beating Wally is to receive from Fred; the Doctor, meanwhile, has had enough, and will only stay long enough to eat and have his horse prepared before travelling on. He has no desire to avail himself further of the Squire's hospitality. [2]

Wally it is, then, who closes the play, which has offered a fine example of how not to behave in polite company, and how not to run a patrician or noble household. As is often the case with such closing speeches in carnival comedies, Wally partially steps out of character to deliver the final message of the piece: a sober address about the value and propriety of respectful self-restraint, and the wisdom of maintaining silence in potentially delicate situations. It is, then, the anarchic fool who not only delivers the conservative moral, but is also seen to learn from his errors and to seek to modify his behaviour - albeit as a response to pain rather than to any more subtle exhortation or abstract stimulus.

The carnival pattern is plain to see: all the elements of mayhem present in the play, and any real threat to the social order, are expressed, contained, and then turned towards a morally useful end. The play is structured not just to restore at its end the *status quo* - an undesirable pattern of behaviour, as the doctor discovered - but to effect salutary change.

---

[2] The audience would no doubt make a link between the size and nature of the Doctor's nose and his evident fondness for food and wine - a fondness which persuades him to stay, albeit temporarily, when his patience has so clearly been exhausted.

The Doctor with the Big Nose

Enter Squire with his groom, Fred:

Good news I hear from far away -
My dearest friend arrives today:
The doyen of the German race,
It will be a joy to see his face.
5   Not just a doctor by degree,
He's also skilled in alchemy;
His violin sounds like a lark,
His bullets never miss their mark;
He is a huntsman brave and bold,
10   And as a diplomat, I'm told,
He always acts with guile and skill
To smooth away potential ill.
Beloved both of prince and peer
He plies his trade both far and near,
15   Is well received wherever he goes
And has no enemies nor foes.
He now takes time to visit me,
To stay with us a day or three.
To talk to one so erudite
20   Will be a thinking man's delight.
We must see he enjoys the best -
He is our most beloved guest.
Treat him with all the skill you can,
As befits a brother nobleman.
25   Do this, and I'll reward you well.

Fred:

Indeed, your Grace, I have heard tell
Of this your friend who comes today -
And he'll not want in any way.
I'll take his muddy boots and gaiters
30   And scrub them clean as new potatoes;
Relieve him of his bags and sword
And treat his horse like an equine Lord:
I'll feed him oats and rub him down.
But wait, your Grace, what of our clown?
35   You know he gabbles like a turkey
And frequently has done some murky
Things for which we've punished him.

Ein faßnachtspil mit vier personen:
Der doctor mit der grossen nasen.

Der junckherr gehet ein mit seinem knecht Fritzen und spricht:
Ich hab durch einen boten vernommen,
Es werd heut ein gast zu mir kommen:
Der künstlichst mann im teutschen land
Beide mit mund und auch mit hand,
5   Ist ein doctor der artzeney,
Auch künstlich in der alchimey,
Artlich auff allem saitenspiel,
Auch rund mit schiessen zu dem ziel,
Zu dem weidwerck kan er auch wol
10   Und was ein hofman künnen sol,
Kan, was gehört zu ernst und schimpf
Und alls höflich mit feinem glimpf,
Ist angnem bey fürsten und herren,
Beide bey nahet und den ferren,
15   Helt sich gantz wol bey iederman;
Ihn sicht doch niemand darfür an.
Derselbig wird mir wonen bey
In dem schloß ein tag oder drey,
Da werden wir zwischen uns beden
20   Nur von artlichen künsten reden.
Den wil ich tractiren auffs best
Als einen meiner lieben gäst,
Den halt du auch ehrlich und wol,
Wie man eren-man halten sol;
25   Daran thust du mir ein wolgfallen.

Knecht Fritz spricht:
Juncker, ja ich wil in ob allen
Ehrlich halten nach ewer sag,
Ihm dienstlich sein, so vil ich mag,
Wil im abziehen die stiffel sein
30   Und die außbutzen wol und fein,
Im auff-hebn watsack, büchsn und schwert,
Mit fleiß versehen im sein pferd,
Mit strewen, strigeln, füttern und trencken.
Doch junckherr, eins ist zu pedencken:
35   Unser narr ist mit worten resch
Und richt offt an gar seltzam wesch;
Wann er stecket vol phantasey,

He thinks that silence is a sin.
I feel he should be locked away.

Squire shouts:

40   Wally, Wally, walk this way!

Wally, the fool, rushes in:

Tell me Gracikins, what's up?
Is it time to share a cup
Of broth, or shall we take a beer?
You look as if you need some cheer!

Squire:

45   Wal, today we have a guest -
Treat him well, do your best.
He is a most important man.

Wally, the fool:

Tell me, what makes him so grand?
If he can cook a decent dinner,
50   Then in my book he is a winner.
If his soup can fill my belly,
Then you know I'll treat him well; he
Can't perchance make a good black pudding?
Hey, when he comes I could en-
55   Quire all about his cakes and buns:
He'll think old Wally's full of fun.
Or does he serve a decent wine?
A muscatel, or a sweet white Rhine,
Or that new stuff from the Harz
60   (That always brings me out in farts!)
If he's that sort, then he's my man.
We'll scoff and drink so neither can
Remember if its March or May.
I hope he comes without delay.

Squire:

65   Wally, you demented lout,
Treat him well, or I'll throw you out!
It's not for you to test his arts,
For he's a man of many parts.
Good God! That's him! I see his banner.
70   Run down and greet him in the sweetest manner!

Und platzt offt ungschwungen in brey.
Verbiet sollichs dem dollen thier!

Der junckherr schreyet:
40   Jäcklein, Jäcklein, kom rein zu mir!

Der Jäcklein rauscht hinein und spricht:
Junckherlein, sag, was sol ich than?
Sol ich den koch heissn richten an?
Hungert dich, so ist dir als mir;
Wenn mich dürst, wer mir auch wie dir.

Der junckherr spricht:
45   Jäcklein, es wird kommen ein gast;
Schaw zu, daß du in ehrlich hast,
Er ist ein künstenreicher mann.

Jäckle, der narr, spricht:
Mein herrlein, sag mir, was er kan!
Ist er seinr kunst ein guter koch,
50   So halt ich in ehrlich und hoch;
Kan er gut feiste suppen machen,
Darmit ich füllt mein hungring rachen,
Gut schweinc-braten und rotseck,
Oder ist er ein semmelbeck,
55   Kan bachen speckkuchen und fladen,
So hab ich seiner kunst gros gnaden;
Oder ist er ein runder keller,
Tregt auff Reinwein und muscateller
Und newen wein in grossen flaschen,
60   Daß ich köndt meinen goder waschen,
Da wolt ich schlemen, fressn und sauffen,
Daß mir augn müsten uberlauffen.
So wer mir warlich lieber er,
Als wen er der künstreichst goldschmid wer.

Junckherr spricht:
65   Jäcklein, Jäcklein, du bist gar grob,
Sprich dem herren preis, ehr und lob,
Und frag nit weiter, was er kan,
Er ist ein künstenreicher mann.
Ietzt komt er. Thut in hof nab gehn
70   Und nemt von im das ros all zwen!

Exit Wally and Fred. Squire alone:

        Indeed, I love the Doctor well,
        But I'm uneasy, truth to tell.
        For, though our friendship's old and dear,
        We've not been in touch for many a year.
75   Let's hope that we can recreate
        The bonds that made us intimate.

Enter Wally, Fred, and the Doctor. The Squire, offering the Doctor his hand:

        A thousand welcomes, dear old friend!
        For much lost time let's make amends.
        There's no-one here I'd rather see
80   Than you, sweet Prince of alchemy.
        Now tell me - how long can you stay?

The Doctor with the big nose:

        It grieves me sore - I must away
        To Bamberg by the morning light,
        But hope to stay with you tonight.
85   Come, let us sit, I'll drink a toast
        To you, dear friend and gracious host.
        But I must be on my way by nine.

Squire:

        Run, Frederick, fetch our best red wine!
        Come sit you down on this fine chair,
90   You'll reach your goal with time to spare.
        Now, tell me all the latest news
        From Italy: what are your views?

Enter the groom, with goblets of wine.
Squire:

        Good Doctor, here's a welcome sight:
        A good red wine with a bit of bite!

Squire drinks. The Doctor with the big nose:

95   And with this wine I drink your health;
        May its richness reflect your wealth.

He drinks:

        It has the nose of Sicily
        Or Tuscany - what can it be?

Sie gehen all beid ab. Der junckherr redt mit im selbst und spricht:
    In viel jarn ich den lieben mann
    Wahrhafftig nie gesehen han;
    Ich frew mich sein bey meinem eid,
    Ich denck wol, daß wir alle beid
75   Etwas vor bey den zehen jarn
    Offt frölich mit einander warn.

Sie gehen beid mit dem doctor ein. Der junckherr beut im die hent und spricht:
    Mein herr doctor, seit mir wilkum
    Zu tausentmal! bin ich ehren-frum,
    So hab ich wahrhafftig in nehen

80   Kein gast von hertzen lieber gsehen,
    Ich laß euch in acht tagn nit hin.

Doctor mit der grossen nasen spricht:
    Mein junckherr, ich gefordert bin:
    Auff morgn muß ich zu Bamberg sein.
    Doch hab ich zu euch kehret ein,
85   Die alten freundschafft zu vernewen,
    Doch muß ich wider, bey mein trewen!
    In zwey stunden gwiß auff sein.

Junckherr spricht:
    Geh, Fridrich, trag auff roten wein!
    Setzt euch, herr doctor, ir habt gut zeit,
90   In neun stunden ir nüber reit.
    Last uns von newer zeitung sagen,
    Was sich im Teutschland zu hat tragen.

Der knecht kommet, bringt ein schewern mit rotem wein. Junckherr spricht:
    Herr doctor, nun seit guter ding!
    Ein starcken trunck ich euch hie bring!
Und trinckt.

Doctor mit der grossen nasen spricht:
95   Mein junckherr, den gesegn euch gott!
    Der wein von farben ist gut rot.

Doctor mit der grossen nasen trinckt und spricht:
    Ich glaub, das sey ein welschwein gut,
    Welchen man den curs nennen thut.

Wally, the fool, bobbing and weaving about, laughs aloud:

Oh dear, oh my, Doc! God bless you!

100   Your hooter's gone a funny hue!
And now I look at it - good Lord!
There's room for seven hens aboard.
What is your name, you wondrous steed?
You must be King of all your breed!

105   Elect among the greatest snouts:
One sneeze and all the lights go out!

The Doctor averts his gaze in embarrassment. Squire:

A pox on you, you witless goat!
Fred! Duck the moron in the moat!

Fred, the groom, bundles the fool outside. Squire:

He cackles like a toothless crone.

110   I'll see that we are left alone.
Sweet Doctor, come and walk with me:
I'll show you all the finery
Of my country seat and my estate!

Doctor:

Indeed, I heard a friend relate

115   The wonders of your new domain,
When I was recently in Spain.

Exit Doctor with Squire. Wally sidles in:

His Lordship said I should behave
More like an angel than a knave,
And praise our guest. Well, as you see,

120   I took myself the liberty
And praised his nose - his bestest bit.
It seemed it pleased him not one whit!
Although I know not what I said,
He choked, he stared, his face went red,

125   As if I'd told some whopping lie.
I didn't even ask him why
His nose was bent and full of bogeys,
All warty and knobbly, like some old fogey's!
Well he clearly doesn't like the truth,

130   So I'll proceed with lies, forsooth,
To see if I regain his favour:
A moment that we both will savour.

Jäckel, der narr, gnipet und gnapet daher, lachet sehr und spricht:
>Kleins herrlein, got gsegn dir dein trincken!
100 Wie hast du so ein schönen zincken,
>Er hat die leng vornen hinauff,
>Es sessn wol siben hennen drauff.
>Ey lieber, nenn dich, wie du heist,
>Ich glaub, der nasen-küng dw seist,
105 Auß allen grossen nasn erkorn;
>Du hast ie ein schönes leschhorn!

Der doctor schemt sich und schawet unter sich. Junckherr spricht:
>Schweig Jäcklein, daß dich die drüs rür!
>Stoß den narrn nauß für die stuebtüer!

Fritz, der knecht, stöst den narren hinauß. Der junckherr redt weiter:
>Er dalet wie ein alte hetz.
110 Wer mag hören sein unnütz gschwetz.
>Mein herr doctor, komt, schawt mein new
>Zirlich und gewaltig gebew!
>Ein schloß bawt ich in jar und tagen!

Doctor spricht:

>Ja, von dem baw so hört ich sagen
115 Weil ich noch war in dem Welschlant,
>Von eim, der euch ist wol bekandt.

Sie gehen all drey ab. Jäcklein schleicht hinein und spricht:
>Mein junckherr sagt, ich solt dem man
>Groß zucht und ehr beweisen than.
>Da sah ich nichts grössers an im,
120 Denn sein nasen, als mich gezim,
>Die im schier zu-deckt sein angsicht.
>Da ich die lobt, gfiel es ihm nicht;
>Wiewol ich im vil ehr erbot,
>Haucht er sich nider, ward schamrot,
125 Als ob ich in het angelogen.
>Hab ich ie die wahrheit anzogen,
>Sein nasen sey bucklet und högret,
>Vol engerling, wümret und knögret?
>Er hört leicht die wahrheit nit gern.
130 Ich wil die sach mit lügn erklern,
>Ob ich wider erlanget huld,
>Hab ie sein feindschaft nit verschuldt.

Enter Fred, the groom:

>　　　Wally, Wally, just stay still.
>　　　His Lordship really doesn't feel
> 135　That you should say another word
>　　　To make the Doctor seem absurd
>　　　And make him blush full beetroot red.

Wally, the fool:

>　　　Ah, Frederick! Kindly boil your head.
>　　　And when you're done, old mate of mine,
> 140　Come kiss me where the sun don't shine!
>　　　No wonder the Doctor feels unsettled,
>　　　With a nose just like a copper kettle!
>　　　If that proboscis doesn't share
>　　　At least first prize at the Autumn Fair,
> 145　I'd like to see the one that wins:
>　　　It would be like a whale without any fins!
>　　　Still, all I've got so far is blows.
>　　　When they come back, let's see how it goes.
>　　　In order to pursue my plan,
> 150　I'll hide the truth from this sensitive man:
>　　　Perhaps I'll even be rewarded
>　　　For making my speech a bit less sordid.

Enter Squire and Doctor. Squire:

>　　　Well, Doctor, how do you like my home?

Doctor:

>　　　It would grace the hills of ancient Rome:
> 155　A very architect's delight!
>　　　I would but that I had all night
>　　　To peruse the assembled finery -
>　　　And to inspect your library!
>　　　It must be better than it was
> 160　Ten years ago, if just because
>　　　The coming of the printing press
>　　　Means good books cost considerably less.
>　　　No doubt you have a few new shelves?

Squire:

>　　　Oh yes! We oft amuse ourselves
> 165　And buy the latest German books,
>　　　Or any other work that looks
>　　　Like fun to read. For just like you,
>　　　My love of literature is true.

Fritz, der knecht, geht ein und spricht:
>   Jäcklein, lieber schweig doch nur still!
>   Der junckherr ernstlich haben will,
> 135 Du sollest gar kein wort mehr jehen,
>   Den doctor zu hönn oder schmehen;
>   Er ist dem junckherrn ein lieber gast.

Der narr spricht:
>   Ey, wie wol dus getroffen hast,
>   Beim ars im schlaff, mein lieber Fritz!
> 140 Kum her und küß mich, da ich sitz!
>   Sag, hat das herrlein nit dermassen
>   Ein grosse rote küpffren nasen,
>   Dergleich ich keine hab gesehen?
>   Hab in zum nasenköng verjehen,
> 145 Weil sein nas war so dick und langk.
>   Hab doch verdient deß teuffels danck:
>   Du stiest mich naus wie einen hund.
>   Wenn sie ietzt wider kehren thund,
>   Wil ich die warheit an den enden
> 150 Dem herrlein fein höflich verquenten;
>   Das wird im leicht gefallen baß,
>   Auff daß er mich zufriden laß.

Der junckherr komt wider mit dem doctor und spricht:
>   Herr doctor, wie gfellt euch mein gebew?

Doctor spricht:
>   Auffs aller-best, bey meiner trew!
> 155 Als obs Lucullus het gebawt,
>   Der Römer, ich habs gern geschawt.
>   Wolt auch geren sehen darbey,
>   Mein junckherr, ewer liberey,
>   Weil ir die seither zehen jar
> 160 Wol bessert habt, glaub ich fürwar,
>   Weil durch den truck seit her, ich sag,
>   Vil guter büchr kamen an tag.
>   Der habt ir on zweiffel ein teil.
>   Ja was von guetn püechern wirt fail
> 165 In teutscher sprach, die kauff ich auff;
>   Hab ir bracht ind liebrey zu hauff,
>   Daran ir ewren lust werd sehen;
>   Wann ich mag in der warheit jehen,

I swear I've known no greater joy
170   Than reading, since I was a boy.
Daily, I enrich my mind
Through contact with the nobler kind -
As befits the questing spirit.

Doctor:

Nobly spoken! Lead me to it,
175   Lead me to this treasure store.

Squire:

We'll dally not a moment more!

Enter the fool. He leans on the Doctor:

You great big floppy gangling man,
Answer me this one if you can!
Where did you get that tiny nose?
180   It looks just like a budding rose,
Or a button on a baby's face!

Doctor, angrily:

Must I put up with this disgrace?
That's twice I've heard the same affront
From this barbaric, smelly runt.
185   I almost regret I came to stay!

Squire:

Fred! Take the bloody fool away.
Beat him with a two-by-four
And leave his brains outside the door!

The groom flings the fool out.

The silly ass should wear a muzzle.
190   Why he talks so is a puzzle.
Rest assured - it's not just you:
Other folks have come to rue
His tongue. But far more pleasant things
Await you in the Library wing.
195   Prayer books, Bibles, philosophy,
The greatest works of history,
And a number of cracking good yarns!

Doctor:

Indeed, I'll overlook the harm
The idiot's tongue has done me here.

Kein grösser frewd hab ich auff erd,
170 Denn zu lesen die bücher werth,
Da ich teglich erfahr das best,
Das ich vor gar nie hab gewest
Als ein ley und unglehrter mann.

Doctor spricht:
Das ist löblich und wolgethan.
175 Nun last mich disen schatz auch sehen!

Der junckherr spricht:
Herr doctor, komt, es sol geschehen.

Der narr tritt hinzu, neigt sich gegen dem doctor und spricht:
Du groß, grader, baumlanger mann,
Ich bit, wöllest mir zeigen an,
Wo hast dein klein näßlein genommen?
180 Von wannen bist du mit her kommen?
Ich main, du habsts eim kind gestoln?

Doctor spricht zornig:
Ey, sol ich sollich schmachred doln,
Die ich nun zweymal hab eingnommen?
Mich rewt schier, daß ich rein bin kommen.
185 Sol ich das leiden von dem gecken?

Junckherr spricht:
Fritz, schlag bald hinauß mit eim stecken
Den narren, daß in drüß ankum!
Der narr ist also tholl und thum.

Der knecht schlegt den narren hinauß. Der junckherr redt weiter:
Er bschnattert alles, was er sicht.
190 Herr, last euch das anfechten nicht,
Der narr thut mir kein dienst daran,
Kein mensch im das abziehen kan.
Komt mit mir in mein liberey,
Da werd ir finden mancherley
195 Bücher, geistlich zu gottes glori,
Philosophey, weltlich histori,
Poetrey, fabel und gut schwenk.

Doctor spricht:
Ja junckherr, ich gleich wol gedenck,
Der narr hab seinr zungen kein gwalt.

200 But this I tell you most sincere -
   One more word, and I'll not stay!

Squire:

   I assure you, Sir, if he should say
   The slightest thing that does you harm,
   Then Fred will tie his legs and arms
205 And beat him till the blood runs down
   To the tips of his toes from the top of his crown.
   You'll hear him howl and wail and plead -
   But come - let's see the Library.

Exeunt. Enter Wally, the fool:

   I don't know what is wrong today.
210 It seems that every word I say -
   And even if it is the truth -
   Means I'm kicked up the arse, forsooth!
   And if I then make free with lies,
   I get the whip on the back of my thighs.
215 This Doctor's not a very big man,
   But he's got a spout like a watering can!
   They always say that little blokes
   Are not very good at taking jokes -
   And this one's driving me quite mad.
220 Both lies and truths seem to make him sad.
   I know now what I've got to do
   To make him see my heart is true.
   I'll tell him that for now, at least,
   I'll leave his wretched nose in peace!

Enter Fred, the groom:

225 Wally, what are you up to now?
   I think you ought to take a vow
   Of silence as regards our guest.
   What you have done is beyond jest.
   And if you don't desist, then I
230 Will beat you till your bowels cry!
   So keep the peace and mind your mouth.

Wally, the fool:

   This Doctor's magnet points due South!
   It is a very odd sort of fellow
   Who hears the truth and starts to bellow.

200   Ich laß gleich gut sein der gestalt,
        Wenn mir dergleich nur nit mehr gschicht.

Junckherr spricht:
        Herr, wenn der narr ein wort mehr spricht,
        Das euch zu einr schmach raichen sol,
        Wil ich dem knecht befelhen wol,
205   Daß er den narrn bind an ein seul,
        Mit rutn haw, biß er wain und heul,
        Daß im das blut herab muß gahn.
        Komt, secht mein liberey fortan.

Sie gehn beid auß. Jäckel, der narr, geht ein, redt mit im selbst und spricht:
        Ich hab zu reden heut kein glück,
210   Es fehlet mir in allem stück:
        Wenn gleich die warheit sage ich,
        So stöst man auß der stuben mich;
        Und kom ich denn mit lügen-sagen,
        So thut man mich mit stecken schlagen.
215   Das herrlein ist an im selber klein,
        Doch ist sehr groß der zoren sein,
        Wie man sagt kleinen männlein vor zeit:
        Der dreck nahend beim hertzen leit.
        So ist dem auch, thut mich bethörn,
220   Mag weder lug noch warheit hörn.
        Botz dreck, was sol ich nun anfangen,
        Deß klein herrleins huld zuerlangen?
        Ich wil halt sagn dem grossen man,
        Sein nasn geh mich gar nichts mer an.

Fritz, der reitknecht, komt und spricht:
225   Sich, Jäcklein, bist du wider hinnen?
        Laß dir fort mehr kein wort entrinnen,
        Das doctors nasen an thw treffen,
        Ihn zu verspotten noch zu effen.
        Ich muß sunst hawen dich mit ruten,
230   Daß dir der rück und ars muß bluten.
        Darumb so hab rhu, allers-narren!

Jäckle, der narr, spricht:
        Ich mein, der doctor hab eins sparrn
        Im kopff zu weng oder zu vil,
        Daß er mich nit vernemen wil.

235 Have I ever said a word
To try and tell him how absurd
His hooter is? I tried to raise
The matter in a spirit of praise:
And, since his snout's the biggest thing
240 Whose gladsome praises I could sing,
How else could I show proper honour
Than via his nose? I bet it's won a
Prize or two. But now I'll cease,
And leave his warty snout in peace.
245 I'm off to tell them what I think.

The groom:

Wally! A nod's as good as a wink.
Don't keep singing the same old song!

Wally, the fool:

Listen, Freddy, something's wrong.
I don't think his conk's his own,
250 'Cos he just never will condone
My comments, be they fair or cruel.
I think perhaps the silly fool
Stole it from the hardware shop,
Or perhaps he stuck this one on top
255 Of his own - to make a real landmark!

The groom:

You mad dog, Wally, must you bark
The same old tune and never cease?
Leave his bloody nose in peace!

The fool:

Oh, come off it! You're just scared!
260 Nothing's gained if nothing's dared.
I'll make the Doctor yet my friend,
And you'll be laughing in the end.
He'll see how innocent I am
And finally will cross my palm
265 With silver, or even yet with gold -
It matches my left eye, I'm told!
Now bugger off, I've things to do.

235 Hab ich doch ie an disem ort
Zu dem herrlein geredt kein wort,
Denn was seinr nasn zu lob und ehr
Reicht, hab gefolgt deß junckherrn ler.
Weil sunst nichts grössers an im ist,
240 Denn sein nasen, hab ich nit gewist,
Was ehr ich ihm erbieten sol,
Denn sein nasen zu loben wol.
Fort wil ich nit mehr loben den,
Wil seiner nasen müssig gehn,
245 Und im das selb auch sagen zu.

Reitknecht spricht:
Mein lieber Jäcklein, sey mit rhu!
Sag von seinr nasen mehr kein wort!

Jäcklein, der narr, spricht:
Hör, Fridlein, ich glaub an dem ort,
Sein nasen kom im nit recht her,
250 Weil darvon nit hört geren er
Reden öffenlich noch verholn.
Er hat villeicht sein nasen gstoln
Dem krämer, der het nasen feil,
Oder hat gar zwen gantzer teil
255 Zusam-gnommen zu einer nasen.

Der knecht spricht:
Jäcklein, thu mit fride in lassen,
Und schweig gar von der nasen stil!
An seiner nassn gwinst nit vil.

Der narr spricht:
Botz dreck! sorgst du, sorg ich doch nit,
260 Deint halb schweig ich nit, ich hoff mit
Das herrlein zu eim freund zu machen,
Daß du mein selbert noch wirst lachen.
So er wird meiner unschuld innen,
Wil ich sein gunst und hueld gewinnen.
265 Er wird mir noch ein paczen schencken,
Den wil ich an mein kappen hencken.
Drumb fetsch dich von mir, laß mich gehn!

The groom:

> I hope that you can really woo
> The Doctor. But you'd best play dumb!
> 270   I hear some talking: here they come!

Enter Squire and Doctor. Doctor:

> A treasure trove indeed, old friend,
> Wondrous books from start to end!
> I never thought you'd have such piles
> Of books - they seem to stretch for miles.
> 275   Reading these, you cannot fail
> To improve your mind, and sail
> Your ship of life on seas so calm,
> Where virtue dispels all alarm.

The fool slaps the Doctor on the shoulder:

> Aye up, Doc! I've got to say
> 280   Your nose don't bother me in any way!
> I don't care if it's big or small -
> I'll never mention it at all!

Squire:

> Fred! Take this damned impertinent dog,
> And tie him up just like a hog -
> 285   Knee to elbow, foot to head -
> Then take him to the lambing shed
> And beat him with a nice thin switch.
> I want to see his backside twitch!

Doctor:

> I feel my presence in this place
> 290   Is not required. I will post-haste
> To Bamberg. Thrice I've now been irked
> By this your fool, who's always lurked
> Behind my back to pull my leg!

Squire:

> Sweet Doctor! Do not go, I beg!
> 295   I've told you more than once tonight
> His bark is far worse than his bite!
> My fool just chatters and jabbers away:
> He never thinks of what he says.
> Everything he sees and hears
> 300   Is made grotesque, and, to our ears,

Reitknecht spricht:

> Ich laß dich dein abenteur bstehn;
> Doch stillschweigen das nützest wer.
> 270 Dort kommens mit einander her.

Sie kommen bede wider. Doctor spricht:

> O junckherr, wie ein thewren schatz
> Habt ir von büchern auff dem platz!
> Solch meng het ich bey euch nit gsucht.
> Gut bücher lesen gibt groß frucht,
> 275 Vorauß wo man darnach richt eben
> Gedancken, wort, werck und gantz leben.
> Denn wird man tugendreich darvon,
> Auch lieb und werth bey iederman.

Der narr klopft den doctor auff die achsel und spricht:

> Herrlein, mich gar nit mehr anficht,
> 280 Du habst ein nasen oder nicht:
> Sie sey geleich groß oder klein,
> Sols von mir unbekrehet sein.

Der junkherr spricht:

> Fritz, nem den narrn ins teuffels namen,
> Und bind im alle viere zsammen
> 285 Mit einem strick, wie einem kalb,
> Zeuch in ab, streich in allenthalb
> Mit einer geschmeissigen ruten,
> Und hör nit auff, biß er thu bluten!

Doctor spricht:

> Mich dünckt, mein sey zu vil im hauß,
> 290 Ich wil gehn machen mich hinauß,
> Weil mich der narr dreymal dermassen
> Mich fretet mit meiner nasen.
> Mich verdreust hart sollichs vexiren.

Junckherr spricht:

> Herr doctor, last euch das nit irren,
> 295 Wie ich euch denn sagt am anfang;
> Wann ider vogel singt sein gsang.
> So thut mein narr reden und kallen
> Alle ding, wie sie im einfallen;
> Auch alles, was er hört und sicht,
> 300 Das lest er unbegeckert nicht,

His unrefined impertinence
Would make a fish seem full of sense!
And though we beat him with a rod
His mind remains bizarrely odd.
305 A brighter man would hold his tongue:
A harder master would have wrung
His neck by now. But take a seat!
Forgive my fool, and come and eat.
There's game and fowl and sundry fish -
310 I know you'll relish every dish!
The chef will see to your every need!

Doctor:

All right. But Fred, prepare my steed!
As soon as I have had my fill,
I make no bones of it, I will
315 Decamp and spend the night elsewhere -
And make my journey on from there.

Exit Squire with Doctor and Fred. The fool, reeling in, closes the play:
A cautionary tale you here do see
Of one whose tongue is all too free,
Who scatters words like leaden shot,
320 Nor cares a fig if they're true or not.
In fact, his goal in life is plain:
To be to one and all a bane!
And if he once should seek the best
And smooth things over with a jest -
325 That's when he does the greatest harm,
Causing general alarm!
No-one's safe when he's about.
He's steeped in mischief, and, no doubt,
Detested by both Lord and knave.
330 He lacks the sense to try and save
Himself from hate on every side -
When silence is all that's required!
To an ancient proverb I'm beholden:
Silence truly can be golden.
335 Had I held my tongue tonight
My bottom would still feel all right.
In future, I will keep the peace
And leave the gabbling to the geese!
I'll even stop my mouth with wax.
340 'A sound idea', says your author - Hans Sachs.

On alle schew und hinderhut.
Darumb man in offt blewen thut.
Doch bleibt er gleich der narr wie vor,
Ein gschwätziger fantast und thor;
305 Wann wer er gscheid, so thet ers nit.
Derhalb, mein herr, so ist mein bit,
Wolt mirs in ubel nit zu-messen,
Und thut zu mittag mit mir essen!
Es ist bereitet schon der tisch
310 Mit wildprät, hasen, fogl und fisch.
Komt nur rein mit mir auff den saal!

Doctor spricht:
Ja wol. Mein Fritz, geh nab in stal,
Strigel und sattel mir das pferd,
Daß nach dem mahl ich gfertigt werd;
315 Wann es ist warlich hhe zeit,
Daß ich heint gen Forchaim reit.

Sie gehen beide ab. Der narr haspelt hinein und beschleust:
Hie nem ein beyspil frau und mann
Bey mir, wer auch nit schweigen kan,
Sunder beschnattert alle ding,
320 Obs gleich schand oder schaden bring;
Es sey auch gleich war oder nicht,
Noch ers auff das spöttlichst außricht,
Darauff hat er am meisten acht,
Wescht für und für gar unbedacht,
325 Wil offt ein sach bessern fürwar,
Und verderbt sie erst gantz und gar,
Und auch keiner person verschonet, -
Wer deß fatzwercks also gewonet,
Wird feindselig bey iederman,
330 Nemt auch vil auf-neschlein darvon,
Ledt auch auff sich vil neid und haß,
Das schweigen im beköm vil baß.
Das alt sprichwort gut kundschafft git:
Mit schweigen verredt man sich nit.
335 Het ich auch gschwigen von der nasen,
So het man mich ungschlagen glassen.
Wil mich nun schweigens nemen an,
Daß ich ungschlagen kom darvon,
Auff daß mir nit ein unglück wachs
340 Auß anderm unglück, spricht Hans Sachs.

Dramatis Personae:

The Squire
The Doctor with the big nose
Fred, the groom
Wally, the fool

Anno salutis 1559, on the 13th day of December.

Die personen dises spils:

1. Junckherr, der edelman.
2. Der doctor mit der grossen nasen.
3. Fritz, der reitknecht.
4. Jäckle, der narr.

Anno salutis 1559, am 13 tag Decembris.

2.   *Peasants and Travelling Scholar, 1560.*

6. THE TRAVELLING SCHOLAR IN PARADISE

Fasnachtspil
Der farent schueler ins paradeis
8 October 1550

The material for this play is found in Pauli's collection of anecdotes, *Schimpf und Ernst*, and elsewhere. [1] Thematically, it echoes the knavery, trickery, and the exploiting of the gullibility of others, found in *Insatiable Greed, The Crying Pup,* and *The Farmer Carrying a Foal,* as well as the marriage theme found in *The Red-Hot Poker, The Crying Pup,* and *Evil Fumes.* Of particular interest here is a variation on the marriage theme: the wife is married for a second time, and it is her nostalgia for an allegedly better first marriage which is the element exploited by the crafty student.

Initially, the wife's lament for her late husband - a simple, pious sort of man - seems touching. Her lot is apparently now far worse, married as she is to what she claims is a miserly second husband. But all is not what it seems, as we shall soon find out. The initial tension, then, is between this seeming lamb of a wife and the wily student, whose initial approach embraces a mixture of boastfulness and wheedling, as he seeks food and a bed. He quickly sums up the wife's vulnerable point - weakness of intellect apart - as being her yearning to do something for her dead husband. His extension of her description of the man, where his bluish hat

---

[1]J. Pauli, *Schimpf und Ernst, 1522,* ed. J. Bolte, 2 vols, Berlin, 1924. See Keller and Goetze, Vol. 14, p. 72 footnote.

becomes *lightning blue* in his 'recollection' is very clever; and the husband's circumstances are described in graphic, heart-rending detail, provide ample testimony to the student's quick-wittedness.

The tension on stage is palpable: will the student dupe the wife before the second husband appears? Both characters on stage desire a quick transaction: he in order to escape, she to ensure the money and the goods reach her first husband in Paradise as soon as possible. A second, delightfully ironic element is introduced by Sachs: the wife, seemingly faithful and virtuous, has, it is revealed, stolen money from the first husband she claims to have loved so dearly, and has hidden it. This is the very money which she now intends to send to him, money which she will replace by similarly robbing her second husband. Sachs strips away the would-be sympathetic portrait of the wife; and now the audience can concentrate on her stupidity, her role as a deceiver being deceived, and the possibility of a well-deserved punishment when the second husband intervenes, as soon he must (line 116).

Introduced as evidently sharper than his wife - he soon sums up what is going on with his 'And now you want to send some things' (line 132) - the husband plays her along by pretending to want to catch up with the student to give him more gifts. Had he shown his true intention right away, his wife might well not have told him where the student had gone. His major outburst once she is off stage - that she is half-witted and will receive a deserved beating once he has dealt with the student - ends with the proverb 'marry in haste, repent at leisure', designed, no doubt, to enlist the connivance and sympathy of at least the male part of the audience, and to elicit a condoning attitude for what he is about to do.

The husband's subsequent fate, of being duped in an even worse fashion by the student than was his wife, can no doubt be particularly savoured by the women in the audience as it unfolds. The husband's efforts to conceal the truth - by asserting he gave the student the horse out of the goodness of his heart, so that the student might get to the first husband all the sooner - work as far as his simple-minded wife is concerned. She is moved to say that she wishes he too could die so that she could send things to him in Paradise. But he realises that the damage cannot be limited to within their household, since his wife has already told the neighbours about sending goods to her first husband; and what she takes as their sharing the fun with her is in fact their mocking her.

The husband's closing speech sees the typically Sachs move towards reconciliation - though many problems remain unsolved, and the loss of clothes and money, indeed the source of the money lost, remains undiscussed between the two. Moreover, the student's criminality is not discussed, being merely represented as an accepted 'fact of life'. In Sachs's equation, however, there can be no room for mutual recrimination when both husband and wife have been so stupid.

Not untypically for the world of Sachs's carnival comedies, the need for marital harmony is a main theme here, as is the need for mutual understanding and support; and, failing all else, the need to recognise that what is sauce for the goose is sauce for the gander. Sachs's message here is very much akin to that in *The Red-Hot Poker*: forgive and forget.

The Travelling Scholar in Paradise

Enter the farmer's wife:

When thinking of the days gone by,
I cannot help but weep and sigh
In memory of my husband dear,
And of a love now disappeared.
5   A simple man and pious too;
It seemed our love just grew and grew.
When he died, joy gave way to pain -
Although I've married now again.
But this one's not quite like my first:
10   He scrimps and saves, and seems averse
To spending any cash at all!
My life is full of bitter gall.
May my first husband rest in peace.
I doubt if I will ever cease
15   To miss him. And I wouldn't haver,
If I could do him one last favour.

Enter the travelling scholar:

Have mercy, mother meek and mild,
On this a hungry, wandering child.
Permit me here to sup and rest,
20   And I will show you how I'm blessed
With knowledge of the finer arts.
I've felt the sting of Cupid's darts
And seen love take men by the collar.
I am, of course, a travelling scholar,
25   Learning, as the world I roam.
Paris is my proper home -
I left there just three days ago.

Wife:

What was that? I didn't know
You came this way from Paradise!
30   Answer me - and be precise -
Did you see my husband there?
He died, and left me full of cares
Just about a year ago.
Alleviate my nagging woe -
35   Is he now one of God's elect?

Travelling scholar:

> Sweet lady, how might I detect
> Your man, among so great a throng?
> What kind of clothing had he on?
> Perhaps I might recall his coat.

Wife:

> 40   I'll tell you what he wore - take note -
> Upon his head a bluish hat,
> Then a winding sheet - and that was that!
> That's how we laid him down to rest.
> It might not seem the very best,
> 45   But that was all he took that day.

Travelling scholar:

> I'd know him from that poor array!
> No breeches, shoes, vest, or shirt,
> His winding sheet all muck and dirt:
> Just like the day you laid him down.
> 50   And sitting there, upon his crown,
> His ancient hat of lightning blue.
> While others order ale and stew,
> He's penniless, and wraps his sheet
> Around his chapped and bleeding feet.
> 55   He's forced to the indignity
> Of living off cold charity.
> That's his role in Paradise.

Wife:

> A man without a single vice,
> Forced to play the pauper's role?
> 60   It grieves me to my very soul
> That he should suffer poverty.
> Tell me, Sir, if you could see
> Your way to going back again?

Travelling scholar:

> Tomorrow I shall start to wend
> 65   My way. It takes me fourteen days.

Wife:

> You'll earn my never-ending praise,
> If you could take my man some things.

Travelling scholar:

> Like Pegasus, I'll soon sprout wings.
> But please be quick - for time flies by!

Wife:

> 70   In the twinkling of an eye
> I'll have a package tied and bound!

Travelling scholar:

> What a stupid fool I've found -
> I wish that there were more around! [2]
> Clothes and money - what a treat!
> 75   At last I'll have some wine and meat.
> I'd best not wait around all day,
> Or her new husband might just flay
> The skin from off my weary back.
> To conning people there's a knack!

Enter wife with a small bundle:

> 80   God speed you, Sir, upon your way!
> These sovereigns I've unearthed today,
> From where I hid them in the byre.
> And now it is my heart's desire
> That you should take them, with this pack,
> 85   And swiftly make the journey back
> To Paradise, to greet my man.
> Stay and tell him, if you can,
> That in the bundle he will find
> Trousers of the noblest kind,
> 90   Shirts and shoes, a coat, some cloth,
> And soon he'll be much better off -
> I'll send him more without delay!
> But Sir, you'd best be on your way,
> The sooner to relieve his pain.
> 95   He is a man without a stain,
> And, of the two, I love him best.

Travelling scholar, taking the bundle:

> I'll gladly do as you request.
> When I reach him he'll dance and shout:
> He'll not be the one left out
> 100   When others drink the night away!

---

[2]The triple rhyme in lines 71-73, present in the original, is most unusual in Sachs's Fastnachtspiele.

Wife:

> Tell me, Sir, how may days
> Must I wait to hear some news?

Travelling scholar:

> I cannot say, for I might lose
> My way on such a winding road.

Wife:

> 105   If that's the case, I ought to load
> Some extra coins into your sack,
> Just in case my man should lack
> For money to enjoy his nights.
> Take him these poor widow's mites -
> 110   For when the harvest's all been sold,
> I'll steal some of my husband's gold
> And hide it in the milking shed -
> Like these, since my first man fell dead.
> Here - take this tip for your own needs,
> 115   And tell my man of my good deeds.

Exit Travelling Scholar. Wife starts to sing. Enter farmer:

> You're the happy one today,
> Old girl - has fortune come your way?

Wife:

> Sit down and hear the circumstance
> That makes me want to sing and dance!

Farmer:

> 120   Something's clearly hit the spot!

Wife:

> Amazing news is what I've got.
> A travelling scholar came my way
> From Paradise, this very day.
> He saw my husband there - my first -
> 125   And swears the poor old man is cursed
> With poverty, and has no shoes
> Nor money for to pay his dues.
> His old blue hat is all he wears,
> And the winding sheet - all tatters and tears.
> 130   I know that's all that he possessed
> The day we laid him to his rest.

Farmer:

And now you want to send some things?

Wife:

My messenger has flown on wings
Of mercy, with a coat and vest,
135   Some boots, and trousers of the best,
A length of cloth, and some small change -
In thanks for what he has arranged.

Farmer:

A noble gesture I must say.
But tell me, dearest wife, which way
140   Did your messenger set out?

Wife:

Of that there's not the slightest doubt!
He set out on the bottom road -
You'll recognise him by his load
And by his yellow neckerchief.

Farmer:

145   Dear wife, you've acted like a thief!
I mean, you've robbed this student blind.
The job he's doing is worth ten times
As much as you are giving him.
Saddle the horse, and I will skim
150   Along the road and tell him so.

Wife:

God bless you, husband, that you show
Such love for my late husband dear!
You know my love for you is sincere:
In death I'll see to your every need!

Farmer:

155   Just hush and pray that our old steed
Catches the lad before the moor -
Once I dismount, he's gone for sure!

Exit wife:

O God! I've got the daftest wife!
Nothing but trouble, toil and strife -
160   A half-wit, cursed with mental gout.
There's none like her for miles about!

This pea-brain, who's so easily led,
Sends clothes and money to the dead!
A year ago her husband dies -
165 And still she falls for this student's lies.
If I can catch him on my horse,
I'll throw him down with such a force,
And rain on him so many blows,
He'll give me back the cash and clothes.
170 And then I'll ride home to my wife
And beat her within an inch of her life!
Her bruises and her two black eyes
Will make her think before telling lies!
She'll ruin me, the silly cow:
175 How I regret my wedding vows!
Marry in haste, repent at ease!
I hope she gets some foul disease!

Wife, shouting from outside:
The horse is waiting in the yard.
You'll catch your man if you ride hard.

Exit farmer. Enter the travelling scholar, carrying the bundle:
180 Dame Fortune's really done her duty:
I've got away with some damn fine booty.
A winter's worth, and no mistake!
These farmer's wives could really make
My life seem just like Paradise:
185 They're gullible, and pay the price!
O God! There's someone after me -
And on a horse - who can it be?
I'll bet that it's the husband, come
To seek me out - I'd best keep mum,
190 And hide my bundle in this bush.
I'll soon be safe, for he can't push
His horse to ride across the moor.
He'll have to tie it up before
He tries to get across that ditch.
195 One more trick and I'll be rich.
I'll hide my yellow neckerchief,
So he won't know that I'm the thief,
And sit and wait here by this tree,
As if expecting company.

Enter farmer, spurring on horse:
200 I say, young man! Young man, I say!

> Did a student pass this way,
> With a yellow kerchief round his neck,
> And carrying a heavy pack
> All wrapped up in a cloth of blue?

Travelling scholar:

205   He was here a minute or two
      Ago - then ran off to those trees.
      Run fast - you'll catch him up with ease.
      Yes! There he is, behind that clump -
      Puffing and panting, and trying to hump
210   His pack through all the undergrowth!

Farmer:

      I bet that's him, upon my oath!
      Young man, look after my old horse,
      While I give chase by foot across
      The moor, and catch the little thief!
215   I'll have him trembling like a leaf -
      He'll beg and plead to be released.

Travelling scholar:

      All right! I'm waiting for a priest
      Who said he'd meet me just near here.
      I'll hold your horse 'til you appear.
220   God speed you on your righteous quest!

Farmer:

      This shilling's yours, if you will rest
      Here and keep hold of my old nag.

Exit farmer. Travelling scholar:

      And now the horse is in the bag!
      With clothes and cash, and now a steed,
225   You've seen to my most urgent needs!
      Today's a really lucky day -
      I can't complain in any way.
      She gives me trousers, shirts, and shoes,
      And him a horse - it's wondrous news!
230   Perhaps he knew my feet were sore,
      And that I'm idle to the core!
      This nag is perfect evidence
      Of neighbourly munificence!
      I bet if he died straight away
235   I'd have another lucky day -

She'd send me off to Paradise,
Not thinking that I'd rob her twice!
Still, time's a-wasting, mustn't stay:
When he comes back, he'll want to slay
240 The cunning author of his woes,
And take back all the cash and clothes.
I'll mount the mare and in a trice
We'll make for our own Paradise -
To drink and eat meat from the spit,
245 While the farmer's up to his knees in shit!

Exits with bundle. Enter farmers's wife:

My husband's been away so long,
I wonder whether something's wrong?
If he's still wandering in the wood,
It won't do my first any good!
250 O Lord! The town bell's signalled three -
It's time my porkers had their tea!

Exit. Enter farmer, looking round:

Oh damn and blast it! Where's my horse?
I should have guessed the truth, of course:
That bastard student's stolen it!
255 He's conned me, and then done a flit,
And taken all the other stuff.
I thought my wife was fool enough -
Now I've been duped just like a child.
Here comes the wife - she's looking riled -
260 I daren't tell her I lost the beast -
Or her respect will be decreased.
Half an hour ago, or less,
I chided my wife's foolishness
In giving this arch-rogue the clothes.
265 Now I deserve a hundred blows
For my arrogant and foul abuse.
I'd better think up some excuse!

Enter wife:

Walking home without the mare?
How did your mercy mission fare?

Farmer:

270 The student said the road was long -
So I thought that it could not be wrong
To lend him our old faithful mare,

90

To help him on his way to where
Your husband waits, in Paradise.
275 I reckoned it would be quite nice
For him to have his horse to ride.

Wife:

To see you show this loving side
Is to see you at your best.
I tell you truly - it's no jest -
280 I wish to God you'd die today,
So you could see the loving way
I'd send a parcel with your clothes
To Paradise. God only knows,
There's nothing that I've hid away
285 I wouldn't send without delay:
Clothes and money, pigs and geese -
The heifers too - you'd never cease
To marvel at my love for you.

Farmer:

Just keep this quiet, whatever you do!
290 Don't boast about your loving labours!

Wife:

Too late! I've gone and told the neighbours!

Farmer:

Must you blurt things straight away?

Wife:

You were barely on your way,
When I ran into the street
295 And told them you were off to greet
My first husband, in Paradise.
They all thought that was very nice,
And shared a little joke with me.

Farmer:

You idiot - why can't you see?
300 They'll hold us up to ridicule!
Dear God! My wife's a bloody fool!
Go inside and make the tea!

Wife:

Husband, I'll go willingly.

Exit wife. Farmer closes the play:

	A man is truly cursed for life
305	Who's saddled with a half-wit wife.
	Her mind's the opposite of deep -
	More on the level of a sheep;
	So gullible, it's not surprising
	That she needs strict supervising.
310	But still, she is a loyal soul,
	And for this deserves her role
	As wife. Although she wastes my time
	And cash, hers aren't the only crimes
	Of stupidness within these walls.
315	For even I can slip and fall,
	When tripped up by a cunning lie.
	Wisdom is in short supply.
	To harmonise as man and wife
	Is the key to a peaceful life.
320	'It's balance the bad marriage lacks -
	Let's hope yours has it', says Hans Sachs.

Dramatis personae:

The travelling scholar
The farmer
The farmer's wife

Anno salutis 1550, on the 8th day of October

3.   *Marital Strife*, 1553?

7. EVIL FUMES

Ein faßnacht-spil mit drey personen
Der böß rauch
13 January 1551

Of all the selection presented in this volume, *Evil Fumes* corresponds most precisely to the standard 'recipe' for a traditional *Fastnachtspiel*, with the husband acting the role of the herald, [1] directly addressing the audience, eliciting their sympathy, and setting up the ensuing action in a narrative, almost Brechtian 'epic theatre' fashion. [2] His plea to the assembled 'gentlemen' to give advice and aid is taken up by his neighbour - presumably emerging from the ranks of those addressed to take part in the play. As was often the case with the carnival comedy, there is a blurring of the distinction between player and audience, play and reality.

The subject matter takes us, and presumably many of the men addressed at the start of the play in particular, into familiar territory - that of the institution of marriage and the highlighting of, or overcoming of, marital difficulties. [3] In this case, we have the situation of the henpecked

---

[1] See E. Catholy, *Fastnachtspiel*, p. 21

[2] See: T. Habel, *Brecht und das Fastnachtspiel*, Göttingen, 1978.

[3] See *The Travelling Scholar in Paradise, The Red-Hot Poker,* and *The Crying Pup.*

husband and the nagging, dominant wife, and the belated determination of the worm to turn, and to demonstrate his virility in a battle to see who shall wear the trousers. [4]

The husband's initial lament - that incessant cajoling from his wife makes his existence a nightmare - is answered by the neighbour's observation that, from the outset, the husband failed to introduce the right discipline into the marriage, and by failing to assert his authority over his wife invited the monstrous domestic regiment under which he now suffers. The contrast with the marriage between Paulina and Philips in *The Crying Pup* is enormous: but parallels between this marriage and the second marriage in *The Travelling Scholar in Paradise*, where the wife is deemed to need strict supervising, are clear; and comparisons between this and the marriage portrayed in *The Red-Hot Poker*, where the wife tries to impose a test of fidelity on her husband, but ends up having her own lack of faith exposed, are illuminating.

Here the fault is clearly underlined as the husband's - though he acted out of love - and the position is evidently irretrievable. But this particular husband cannot resist trying to change a situation which, we learn later in the play, has lasted some thirty years: a splendid example of the triumph of hope over experience. The neighbour, of course, has a foolproof plan: a physical battle to re-establish the proper order of things. The wife's contemptuous dismissal of the husband's proposal is to be expected; her obscene gestures both play to the audience's baser sense of humour and, for those standing rather more aloof from the action, underline the extent to which this wife defies the accepted order by holding her husband in such evident contempt. In this context, her speech in lines 95-103 is interesting. To whom is she addressing herself? To an audience

---

[4]The theme of the 'battle for the trousers' was later to be taken up by Grimmelshausen. See H. J. C. von Grimmelshausen, *Lebensbeschreibung der Erzbetrügerin und Landstörtzerin Courasche*, ed. W. Bender, Tübingen, 1967. Chapter 7 describes Courasche's own battle.

of 'real men' with firmly-established control over their wives? To a mixed audience with a variety of marital relationships? To a 'sisterhood' of domestic amazons? To a Judy element waiting for her to beat up her Punch?

Action soon takes over from reflection in this, by far the most physically active and physically humorous play in this selection - and the battle is quickly over, with the husband prostrate and pleading. The wife is not content with her victory, even though to gain it she has ignored any niceties such as rules of combat, and takes what might be seen as unfair advantage of her situation to escalate the confrontation. Having evicted her husband, she now throws the contents of a chamber-pot over his head as he sits disconsolately outside on the step. [5]

The lie which the husband now feels obliged to propagate in order to attempt to conceal his defeat from the neighbour is exposed as the neighbour rushes in to try to quell the domestic fire: again, there is much business for the actors with water. The conversation between two defeated men (what sort of man cannot prevail against the weaker sex? - asks the cowed neighbour of the husband) is delightfully economical in the way it allows Sachs to expose the weakness of both men, with the husband in particular complaining feebly that the wife struck while he was trying to sort out the rules of combat.

The neighbour attempts to engineer what might be seen as a classic Sachs solution - exhorting the wife to forgive and forget, attempting to restore stability and order. She, however, escalates the situation by demanding from her husband the symbols of his manhood - his knife and purse - and threatens to bar him from his own home if he refuses. The 'knife and purse' refrain is repeated three times in quick succession, as if

---

[5]The staging of the water-throwing scenes in this play requires much thought, particularly if real water is to be used. Equally, the business with the red-hot poker in the play of that name requires either careful mime or recourse to a naturalistic element which is on the whole foreign to the staging of carnival comedies.

Sachs wishes to emphasise the unacceptable lengths to which the wife is going. The sight of the husband capitulating 'in front of all these folk', in other words in front of the audience, who are helplessly witnessing this degrading spectacle, is truly pathetic. Although the neighbour utters thoughts which may be passing through the minds of many men in the audience - 'You must like being sat upon! Have you completely lost your wits?' - he is conveniently chased off stage by the wife, leaving the husband to reveal, at this belated stage, that he has now suffered some thirty years of being dominated thus by his wife. This is a shocking moment, and it merges into the husband's direct appeal to the young men in the audience to rein in their wives, impose their will, and demand obedience. Their marriages will, as a result, remain a strong and working, if unequal partnership. Above all, some semblance of good order will be preserved, and the fabric of society will not be damaged.

Sachs's chief concern here is evidently to underline the fact that stable marriages form the bedrock of a stable social order, that failure on the part of the man to establish a 'proper' working relationship between himself and his wife is reprehensible, and that this can lead to mis-rule on the part of the wife: a highly undesirable mode of existence.

Evil Fumes

Husband enters and bows:

        I bid you welcome, goodly Sirs,
        And ask of you to lend your ears
        To my complaint about my wife,
        Who makes a nightmare of my life.
5   By day, by night, at meals, in bed,
        Curses rain down on my head.
        She nags and harries me, and cajoles:
        I've got indigestion of the soul.
        Barely have I swallowed one,
10   Than another insult clouds my sun.
        Thinking how a marriage ought to
        Be, my eyes will fill with water.
        And when she brings me to my knees
        I often think a mild disease
15   Would let me rest a day or three!
        But she's relentless, as you'll see,
        And gives me not a second's peace.
        If only I could be released
        And have a life of tranquil ease!
20   And so I beg you, Gentlemen, please,
        Give me your advice and aid.

Neighbour:

        I've listened to each word you've said;
        But it's just too late to complain.
        You gave your wife too slack a rein
25   To start with, and she soon observed
        Your foolishness, and had the nerve
        To want to dominate your house.
        Now she's the lord and you're the mouse.
        The fault must lie at your own door!

Husband:

30   You tell the truth and nothing more,
        O neighbour! I was far too kind:
        I should have curbed her ways in time.
        But I loved her, and I stood and stared
        In wonderment, while she prepared
35   To subjugate this guileless man:
        And not once did I raise my hand!
        And since that cruel and fateful start
        I've played the fool with a broken heart.

40   I would only court disaster
In trying to prove that I'm the master:
They'd all mock me at the inn.

Neighbour:

We all know that you have to grin
And bear it, and that you're obliged
45   To play the fool and weep inside.

Husband:

I'm begging of you, dear old friend,
Show me how to put an end
To this disgrace, and be a man.

Neighbour:

Dear neighbour, here's a foolproof plan.
50   Fortify your quaking heart;
Tell your wife that you will start
By offering to have a fight
To see which one should have the right
To wear the trousers in your house.
55   The one who proves victorious
Will henceforth have the sole decree
Over things that shall or shall not be.
This is the best and quickest scheme!

Husband:

I'm still uneasy, for it seems
60   My victory is not assured.
My wife's a devil and I'm a fraud,
As men go. But we'll try your way.

Neighbour:

Your wife is coming, don't delay!

Enter wife. Exit neighbour. Husband:

Listen wife! I've had my fill
65   Of you as Jack and me as Jill:
I just won't stand it any more!

Wife:

Well, lay yourself down on the floor
And wave your legs up in the air!

Husband:
>   I've warned you, wife! You'd best beware -
> 70   Pretty soon you'll feel my fist.

Wife makes obscene gesture:
>   Husband, tie a knot in this
>   Then go and sit down on a spike!

Husband:
>   That's not the kind of talk I like.
>   You'll bow to my authority!

Wife makes a different obscene gesture:
> 75   How many fingers can you see?

Husband:
>   I'm going to reassert myself!

Wife:
>   I hear the squeaking of an elf!

Husband, becoming more angry:
>   My patience now is at an end,
>   You'd best decide that you will bend
> 80   Your will to mine and I will rule.

Wife:
>   I've always thought you were a fool,
>   And nothing now will change my mind.

Husband:
>   If that's the case, then we must find
>   A way to settle who shall wear
> 85   The trousers here. So if you dare,
>   We'll have a fight to sort it out.

Wife:
>   I see no need to beat about
>   The bush. Run out and fetch a brace
>   Of clubs, then we'll stand face to face
> 90   And beat each other black and blue.
>   The winner then will claim what's due,
>   And rule this house for ever more.

Husband:

We'll make that an unbending law!
I'll go and fetch two wooden staves.

Wife:

95   My wretched husband clearly craves
A beating. He lacks guts and heart.
I'll see he soon regrets his part
In this! I know he fears my tongue:
He'll fear the rest when I have wrung
100   His neck and put him in his place.
The poor fool faces sure disgrace.
A man who flinches when I shout
Will run away after one good clout!

Enter husband with two cudgels:

These cudgels are of equal length;
105   Take your pick and try your strength -
And don't hold back on my account.

Wife snatches one of the cudgels:

No husband! I have any amount
Of energy to spend on you!
I'll beat you till your arse turns blue!
110   You'll barely live to tell the tale!

Husband hangs up the trousers:

I'll hang the trousers on this nail,
Then we'll draw lots to let us know
Who shall strike the very first blow.

Wife starts to hit him:

I'm not bound by any rules!
115   Save yourself, you stupid fool!

She hits him; he runs away, and puts up some token resistance, and then runs again; she knocks him to the ground. Husband, raising both hands:

Spare me, wife, you've won the bet!
Your fighting skills make me regret
I ever sought to challenge you.
From you, dear wife, I'll take my cue:
120   I'll stay at home and sit and spin,
Sweep the floor, take washing in,
Rake the ashes in the hearth,

And cook and clean for all I'm worth.
And never once I'll raise my fist.

Wife:

125   I'd make you very soon desist
If you once had the nerve to dare!
But, since I beat you fair and square,
I order you to leave this house.
Run along, you little louse,
130   Or else I'll spank you on your nappy
And really make you feel unhappy.

Exit husband. Wife, picking up the breeches:
So now I've made the breeches mine
And forced my man to toe the line.
He's sitting on the steps out there:
135   I think it's time I washed his hair -
With water from the washing up!
And when he feels his little cup
Of woe is filled up to excess -
This chamber pot will make more mess!

Exit. Enter husband, who sits down sadly:
140   O God! What sort of wife is this?
She leaves her man not with a kiss
But with a body sore and bruised,
Put to flight and all confused.
I felt the thunder of the pain,
145   And then the misery of the rain!

Enter neighbour:
Good neighbour, why this sullen face?
And isn't this a funny place
To sit? And why are you wet through?
Tell me, neighbour, tell me do!

Husband, angrily:
150   We had a sudden chimney fire -
It could have been our funeral pyre!
I doused the flames and got wet through:
The evil fumes then forced me to
Escape and seek some good fresh air.

Neighbour:
155   I'm disappointed you don't care
   Enough to ask me for my aid.
   I'll go inside and check you've made
   The fire safe, and saved your home.

Husband:
   Good luck! I'll let you go alone.
160   I think I'll rest here for an hour.

Exit neighbour. Husband follows him:
   I'll bet he gets a sudden shower!
   Perhaps I'll tag along behind
   And see the welcome that he finds!

Husband sidles out. Enter wife:
   The drowned rat sitting in the yard,
165   Complaining that his life's too hard,
   Was my man. Now he is my fool.
   He'll never seek again to rule
   This house. But wait, he's coming back.
   My chance to give him one last whack!

Enter neighbour with a bucket of water. Wife attacks him. Neighbour:

170   Neighbour, why this show of ire?
   I've come to help you douse your fire!
   Your husband said your hearth's ablaze.

Wife:
   Get out of here before I raise
   More lumps on you, instead of him!
175   You shouldn't stick your muzzle in
   Where it's not wanted. Disappear!
   Before I come and box your ears!

Neighbour:
   I'm off! No need to raise your hand.
   And now I'm sure I understand
180   The source of all those 'evil fumes'.

Exit neighbour. Wife:
   No doubt my husband now assumes
   I'm done with him - but that's not true!

I think I'll send another brew
Of nectar pouring from the skies -
185   Oh, won't he have a nice surprise!

Exit wife. Enter husband:
The one good thing to come of this
Is now my neighbour also fears
My wife. I saw him run and hide
When he felt the wrath of the distaff side!

Enter neighbour:
190   Neighbour! You're a common liar!
You tricked me with your tales of fire.
Your chimney wasn't half as hot
As the awful beating that I got
From your dear wife! You must confess,
195   Your manliness grows less and less.
How could you challenge her and fail?
What sort of man cannot prevail
In combat with the weaker sex?

Husband:
She launched a series of attacks
200   Whilst I was trying to set out
The rules of combat for our bout!

Neighbour:
But didn't you strike back at all?

Husband:
I just had strength enough to crawl
Away, so wild was her assault.
205   Four blows to one! I soon called halt.
And then the lights began to dim,
As she attacked my every limb.
Finally, I begged her stop.

Neighbour:
If I were you, I wouldn't drop
210   The matter yet. Fight her again!
If you inflict a little pain,
She'll see who's lord and master here!

104

Husband:

<blockquote>
It's much too late for that, I fear!
Before I go another round
215   With her, and feel the cudgel pound
My bones, I'll let her have her way
And wear the trousers, night and day.
But will she ever have me back?
</blockquote>

Neighbour:

<blockquote>
You'll live in fear of more attacks!
220   She's coming! Let me handle this.
</blockquote>

Wife:

<blockquote>
So there you are! Well, what's amiss?
Do you want another taste?
</blockquote>

Neighbour:

<blockquote>
Why, dear neighbour, do not waste
Your anger so. I wish to ask
225   If you will drop this manly mask
And be a nice obedient wife.
</blockquote>

Wife:

<blockquote>
I'll do what I've done all my life.
Why should I change my habits now?
I'd have to be a silly cow!
230   And anyway - is this your fight?
</blockquote>

Neighbour:

<blockquote>
No neighbour - but I have the right
To ask you to forgive your man
And take him back - he's like a lamb!
</blockquote>

Wife:

<blockquote>
I think I must be hearing things!
235   A lamb who barks and tries to win
The trousers that I've worn for years!
</blockquote>

Neighbour:

<blockquote>
A lamb who cries heartrending tears.
Do not let your bitterness
Drive out your loving tenderness;
240   Forgive your man and then forget -
Or you'll both have much to regret.
</blockquote>

Wife, holding up trousers:
>These are mine - I won the fight.
>But if that stupid fool is quite
>Prepared to grovel to his wife,
>245 Then let him come with purse and knife
>And kneel and tie them round my waist.
>Then perhaps he'll lose his taste
>For dispute and leave me alone
>To rule. If not, he'll lose his home.

Husband clasping his hands together:
>250 Your husband on his knees beseeches:
>Take no more! You've won the breeches.
>Leave me with my knife and purse,
>Or life will be a dreadful curse!
>As it is I'll have to hide,
>255 Lest others scornfully deride
>My plight. Just take me back, I plead!

Wife:
>Shut your mouth! I'll pay no heed
>To your lament. Just one more word,
>And you will surely have to gird
>260 Yourself to fight for purse and knife.

Wife hangs up the breeches. Husband:
>I've had enough of futile strife!
>The pain can only get much worse
>If I defend my knife and purse.

Neighbour:
>O neighbour! Don't give up this chance!
>265 If I were you, I'd make her dance
>To a different tune! Just have a go!

Husband:
>Since you're so keen to strike a blow,
>Step up here and take my place.
>And if you wipe out my disgrace
>270 A dozen sovereigns are your prize!

Neighbour:
>Oh no! Not me! I've seen the size
>Of that great cudgel in her fist!

One blow and I'll see purple mist!
No! I'm off home, I've had enough.

Husband unbuckling his purse and knife, handing them to his wife:

275 Dear wife, for me you are too rough.
My purse and knife belong to you.

Wife:

Put them on me, husband, do!
Here, in front of all these folk -
Then they'll see you are a joke.
280 You know I've won with might and main -
You'll never challenge me again.

Husband, buckling purse and knife on her:

Anything for you, dear wife!
Anything for a quiet life!
I'll help you put your breeches on.

Neighbour:

285 You must like being sat upon!
Have you completely lost your wits?
Give her a couple of hefty hits
About the ears, you silly sod!

Wife:

I'll make you eat those words, by God!

Neighbour flees. Wife pursues him. Husband:

290 Her death would bring me sweet salvation
After so much tribulation
Over these past thirty years!
You young men, lend me your ears!
From the start, employ your skill -
295 Persuade your wife obedience will
Be the best path. Should she refuse,
Impress on her her wifely dues,
And let her see your earnestness.
If she then still fails to address
300 Her given role, then, in due course,
You punish her - but show remorse.
They say a man who's truly pious
Can shape his marriage without bias.

My fault lay in my own neglect:
305   My wife's free rein was never checked.
The outcome now? Our marriage vows
Dissolved in bitterness and rows.
'The vital things their marriage lacks
Are love and concord', says Hans Sachs.

Dramatis personae:

The evil wife
The husband
The neighbour

Anno salutis 1551, on the 13th day of January.

4. *Between God and Mammon*, Niklas Stör?, 1530?

8. INSATIABLE GREED

Faßnachtspiel mit 5 personen
Der unersetlich geitzhunger
5 September 1551

The 'Insatiable Greed' of the title characterises what Sachs sees as the driving force behind the unacceptable face of capitalism, a portrayal of which constitutes the core of this play. [1] Here we see how the grasping Lux Reichenburger - what a splendidly evocative name for a rich fraudster! - and his crooked wife seek to swindle Simplicius. Although a more acceptable face of trade and business is represented by the sympathetic figures of Simplicius -a guileless, upright, honest man, who makes a living in the world of moneylending and commerce - and through his wise and worldly friend Sapiens, Sachs's principal concern in this play, where the characters' names act as unusually clear moral signposts, seems to be to warn against the kind of sharp practice and moral bankruptcy associated with an over-zealous pursuit of wealth. Given Sachs's own status as a property-owning and highly reputable tradesman and citizen, this theme may be assumed to have been close to his heart.

Simplicius's opening speech affords thought-provoking insights into the state of banking and the practice of money-lending in Sachs's time

---

[1]See I. Spriewald, *Literatur zwischen Hören und Lesen. Wandel von Funktion und Rezeption im späten Mitelalter*, pp. 149-59; and R. E. Schade, *Studies in Early German Comedy*, pp. 93-94.

(there being no indication that the play is set in any other era). Simplicius has apparently taken a considerable risk in lending money and feels fortunate to have recovered the debt in full and at the debtor's own initiative. Trusting though he is, he will not carry the cash around with him for fear of robbers. A bank is apparently not available (though modern-style exchange banks did exist by this time), so Simplicius decides to turn to an established, property-owning citizen who can temporarily safeguard the money. Sachs rapidly establishes the trusting nature of Simplicius, and his characterisation of Lux is equally swift and sure. We see Lux lamenting a drop in income from his mines, his farm, and his factory, and from the fact that he has now ceased to act as a guardian. He complains that he cannot invest his spare money, as nobody will give him nine per cent return. There are repairs to carry out in the home, and thus economies must be made, although we know that he still enjoys a sizeable income and has spare money to invest. Lux's recipe for economic survival in these moderately straightened circumstances is to tell his wife to cut back on essentials and to make the servants suffer as well: an early example of the trickle-down effects of recession. Sachs allows us seemingly realistic glimpses of everyday life as Lux debates what to do; the stove is to be fixed, the walls need painting, and the windows must be re-glazed. And all the while the servants are stealing clothes from Lux and his wife, and damaging goods. The wife's recommends that Lux raise his interest rates; he retorts that he does so constantly, and feels no compunction in that respect, since his heart is made of stone. The picture of the pair is decidedly unedifying. It is interesting to note that, yet again in a Sachs carnival comedy, the image of the wife is that of a distinctly tarnished creature: although, in this case, a particularly mercenary Eve leads an all-too-willing Adam into what is for them a pretty familiar sin. It is unto this pair of hard-hearted, grasping usurers, then, that Simplicius is about to entrust a considerable sum of cash.

When Simplicius arrives and explains his need, as an itinerant merchant speculator, to find a safe temporary home for his cash, Lux feigns reluctance but accepts the responsibility. His criminal instinct and that of this wife are aroused when the trusting Simplicius departs without demanding a written receipt for the money, which is contained in a sealed bag. Sachs clearly highlights two differing codes of capitalist behaviour as represented by Simplicius, on the one hand, for whom a man's word is his bond, and Lux and his wife, on the other, ready to take criminal advantage of Simplicius's trusting ethos. The parallels with late twentieth-century developments are striking.

Lux does seems to retain some vestiges of decency, as he points out to his wife that the two of them are courting disgrace. But Sachs goes on to make clear that fundamentally it is the fear of exposure that worries Lux, and he is not motivated by any sense of moral decency. His wife, indeed, reveals that a little dishonesty has never worried either of them previously, so why should this planned major deceit cause them to have furrowed brows? Furthermore, they calculate that their good reputation, gained, it seems, despite the reality of their dishonesty, will protect them from any suspicion of wrongdoing. The last of their calculations - involving an estimation of the effect such a course of action would have on their souls - is quickly done. On Judgement Day, it seems, there will be any number of cheating moneylenders facing the same fate; Lux and his wife are happy to opt for a 'safety in numbers' policy, which is, of course, a gross self-deception and flies in the face of Lutheran doctrine.

As is not infrequently the case in his carnival comedies, Sachs moves the drama along at a considerable pace by eliding the whole of Simplicius's business trip abroad and having him 'return' at the end of the passage of dialogue where Lux and his wife are pondering and planning: no time lapse is indicated. The confrontation between the Reichenburgers and Simplicius is kept uncomplicated. Accusing the pair of cheating him, Simplicius is in turn accused of inventing the entire episode and is threatened both physically and with the law. In modern parlance, this is a splendidly-portrayed 'sting'.

A despondent Simplicius, now facing the bitter truth of his loss, has his prayers answered as he runs into his old friend Sapiens on the street: again, there is no pretence at realism here from Sachs. Simplicius is chided for his naivety in not obtaining a receipt for his money, and Sapiens sets about devising a ruse to get Simplicius his money back - a ruse which will depend on Lux's greed for an even bigger prize bringing him to surrender Simplicius's cash to its rightful owner. Lux will be hoisted with his own petard.

The audience is now treated to a little play within a play, a device Sachs frequently uses in his carnival comedies, [2] as an elderly jewel merchant and Simplicius contrive to fool Lux and his wife into accepting a casket full of straw and gravel and fake jewels, having pressured him into giving back Simplicius's money in order to gain the bigger prize. The biter is well and truly bit.

The final message delivered by Sapiens is simple: trade should only be conducted with and between men of honour with a sound public reputation. Sachs rounds off the play with a conservative Christian homily, warning against becoming enslaved to and corrupted by greed for material goods - praying to Mammon, in other words - an ethic which the respectable citizen and master cobbler must have felt was fundamental to his own way of life.

---

[2]See also Chapter 10, p.141, and Chapter 13, p. 189, for other instances of plays within plays.

Insatiable Greed

Enter Simplicius, a guileless man:
    Good fortune's on my side today!
    A debtor here has just repaid
    In full, and of his own volition,
    Cash I lent on strange conditions
5   Round about two years ago.
    And so I've reaped all that I sowed.
    I do confess to being astounded
    That my worries proved unfounded.
    But I still must find a local place
10   Where I'll know that all this cash is safe.
    I dare not carry it about,
    For fear of robbers: I've no doubt
    That prying eyes are everywhere.
    There's someone, though, who'd be prepared
15   To act as a custodian
    Until I can come back again,
    And keep my money held in trust:
    Lux Reichenburger would be just
    The man - a citizen, like me.
20   Let's hope he'll act as my trustee.

Exit Simplicius. Enter Lux Reichenburger:
    Oh dear, oh dear, this life is tough!
    All my efforts aren't enough
    To counteract the fickleness
    Of fortune: and, to my distress,
25   I've suffered greatly this past year.
    My mining operation here
    Collapsed; I've sold my factory;
    The price of corn falls every day;
    And I've lost a steady little wage
30   Now my ward has come of age.
    I've got a thousand sovereigns spare,
    But no-one out there seems prepared
    To give me nine per cent return.
    And trade's so slack I've hardly earned
35   A thousand this past year and more.
    So much hard work to stay so poor!
    If things continue I'll go bust -
    Then how am I to earn a crust?

Enter his wife:

> Husband, empty out your pocket:
> 40   I need some money for the market.
> Hurry up! The clock's struck two.

Reichenburger:

> I'd like to know just what you do
> With my cash - you had some last week!

Wife:

> And spent it buying bread and leeks
> 45   And meat and things a household needs.
> You seem to think food grows on trees!

Reichenburger:

> To Hell with that. Now here's a tip:
> You need to get a tighter grip,
> And be less spendthrift in your ways.

Wife:

> 50   I scrimp and save from day to day.

Reichenburger:

> Well, make the servants suffer too!
> There's lots of building work to do:
> Glazing windows, painting walls -
> The stove still needs an overhaul.
> 55   Who's to pay, I'd like to know?

Wife:

> There's no need to worry so.
> Put the rates up on your loans.

Reichenburger:

> I do it all the time. I've stone
> Where other people have a heart.
> 60   Our servants, though, are getting smart:
> Last week the ostler stole a coat
> From me, and that sticks in my throat.

Wife:

> My maid has stolen my new vest
> And night-cap: it's beyond a jest.
> 65   If I find them, she'll pay dear.

I've had to fine her twice this year
For dropping dishes on the floor.

Simplicius knocks. Reichenburger:
>Go and see who's at the door.

Enter Simplicius with his bag of money:
>Good Sir, I come to you in trust.
70 Along with friends of mine, I must
Soon make my way to the Lyons fair.
May I entrust to your good care
These thousand sovereigns which today
I earned from a debt that's been repaid?
75 I rarely ask for such a favour,
But, seeing you, I shall not haver.
If God is willing I'll be back
In two months to collect my sack.

Reichenburger:
>I hesitate to take your gold
80 When on mine I have a precarious hold!

Simplicius:
>Do your best on my account
And I'll give your wife a small amount!

He hands her some money. Reichenburger:
>You plead your case with eloquence:
I'll do it for you just this once.

Simplicius:
85 Take the sack - the seal's unbroken -
The money's all there, by my token.
You see a man who's much relieved!

Reichenburger:
>I wish you fortune and God speed!

Exit Simplicius. Reichenburger:
>What are we supposed to do?

Wife:
90 He gave me money: maybe you
Will get some, if he's satisfied.
But I've a little thought inside

My head: what if our friend should meet
With an accident on some dark street?
95   We'd keep the lot - and our own son
Could have a wedding second to none,
If he should choose to take a wife.

Reichenburger:

His kinsfolk would create such strife
We'd have to hand the money over.

Wife:

100   But who's to tell where such a rover
Put his cash to keep it safe?

Reichenburger:

He seemed to have a childlike faith -
Naïve and simple in approach.
He didn't even try to broach
105   The subject of a signed agreement.

Wife:

Listen closely now: when he went
He left without a written contract.
If he tries to get his cash back,
Say you've never seen his face!

Reichenburger:

110   A clever ruse - but we court disgrace
If we're to stoop to what you've just
Described: we'll forfeit people's trust.
Our friend may ruin our repute.

Wife:

Folks know you're honest and astute.
115   You're respected - he's a stranger;
There won't be the slightest danger
People here might take his word.
The very thought is quite absurd!
And, if the case should go to court,
120   Your friends will say you're not that sort:
The stranger will soon get short shrift!

Reichenburger:
>A sack of gold is quite a gift.
>Still, though it's nice, what is the cost
>If our faith is doubted, our honour lost?

Wife:
>125   You've never had a furrowed brow
>About such things - why worry now?
>Honour grows in line with wealth.
>You'll never be accused of stealth
>Or subterfuge - no-one would dare!

Reichenburger:
>130   Here's another worry I must share:
>Won't our mortal souls be affected?

Wife:
>On Judgement Day, when they're inspected,
>We'll all be on the same agenda:
>Every cheating moneylender.

Reichenburger:
>135   You seem at your persuasive best
>Dear wife. Let's put it to the test.

Wife:
>Nothing ventured, nothing gained.
>A thousand sovereigns are worth the pain.
>Look how they glisten through the sack!

Simplicius knocks. Reichenburger:
>140   Good God! The door is being attacked.

Wife, looking out:
>It's him! He's come back for his gold!

Reichenburger:
>Well, don't make him stand there in the cold.

Enter Simplicius:
>God save all here, as he's assisted
>Me to come back unmolested!

Reichenburger:
>145   How may I assist you, Sir?

Simplicius:

> By paying back, without demur,
> The gold entrusted to your care:
> A thousand golden sovereigns fair!

Reichenburger:

> A thousand what? You must be dreaming.

Simplicius:

> 150   The sack of gold I left here, deeming
> You a man discreet and just.

Reichenburger:

> You seem confused, I think you must
> Have left it with the man next door.

Simplicius:

> Your wife was there and clearly saw
> 155   Our business. Is that not the case?

Wife:

> I swear I've never seen your face.
> On that you have my solemn word.

Simplicius:

> How can you say that? It's absurd!
> You had from me a handsome gift!

Wife:

> 160   I think, Sir, that you are bereft
> Of reason, or have lost your bearings.

Simplicius:

> Oh, now I see it! We're all sharing
> A little joke about my gold.

Reichenburger:

> Listen, stranger, you've been told
> 165   We've never seen you: you're a cheat!
> I'll throw you out into the street
> If you don't leave here right away!

Simplicius:

> Then I'll go straight to the mayor and say
> You've cheated me of what is mine.

Reichenburger:

170   It's up to you how you waste your time.
For all your knavish trickery
You'll end up under lock and key!

Exit Simplicius. Reichenburger:

The prize is almost ours! But then -
He's not the wiliest of men!

175   Simple by nature and simple by name:
He truly is an innocent lamb.
Let's go down to the barn again
And check on our supply of grain.

Exeunt. Enter Simplicius, sadly:

How can I pursue my cause

180   When Lux defies me and ignores
My pleas? I need a trusted friend
To help me reach a happy end.
Someone's approaching! If by chance
It were Sapiens, I'd sing and dance.

185   My dearest friend! It's him indeed!
He'll give me all the help I need!

Enter Sapiens:

Simplicius! What brings you here?
You've had some accident, I fear:
I've never seen you look so glum.

Simplicius:

190   I'm tangled up in a rum
Affair: I don't know what to do.

Sapiens:

Then let me be of help to you -
Share your burden with a friend.

Simplicius:

I always knew I could depend

195   On you. The whole predicament
Is that two months ago I lent
Lux Reichenburger a sack of gold
In trust, for him to have and hold
Until I should return again

200   From Lyons, and make my proper claim
On what was mine. But, faced with me,

He now denies he's ever seen
My money, and calls me a cheat.
He tried to throw me into the street.
205   So what should be my course of action?

Sapiens:

Was the original transaction
Signed and sealed in your own hand?

Simplicius indicates it was not.

Sapiens:

Then Reichenburger should be damned!
Was no-one witness to the deal,
210   To whom you now could make appeal?

Simplicius:

None except his own dear wife,
Who now will swear upon her life
She too has never set eyes on me.
Sapiens: how should we proceed?

Sapiens:
215   You made a most unwise mistake
When you allowed this man to take
Your cash, without signing his name
To force him to accept your claim.

Simplicius:

Indeed, I placed far too much trust
220   In appearances. I fear I must
Have been taken in by his noble airs
And his splendid array of costly wares.
He seemed the best of townsfolk here.

Sapiens:

Appearances have cost you dear.
225   If asked about his reputation,
I could have made a compilation
Of all the recent tricks he's played -
Which have no place in honest trade.
But no-one dares to say a thing.
230   His avarice is frightening:
Folk avoid him if they can.

Simplicius:

          Tell me: what should be my plan?
          Should I take him straight to court?

Sapiens:

          But you've no proof of any sort,
235   No witness, nothing he has signed.
          The cheating Devil's robbed you blind.
          And, even if you have a case,
          He'd swear you're lying, to save his face.

Simplicius:

          If my money's really lost,
240   Then someone's going to pay the cost
          And get a knife right through the heart!

Sapiens:

          Patience is the key! Don't start
          To lose it - it's your one great gift.
          I have a friend who'll help us lift
245   The burden off your heart and mind.
          He trades in gems, of the exotic kind,
          And knows old Lux. What if he asked
          Our Lux to do the simple task
          Of guarding, as a trusted friend,
250   A little cask that he'd pretend
          Was full of jewels - whereas, you see,
          It was full of stones, put there by me?
          Then just as they were shaking hands
          You'd come in, just like a lamb,
255   And gently ask for your money back:
          The thousand sovereigns in the sack.
          For fear of frightening off my friend,
          He might change his mind and lend
          A kindly ear to what you ask.
260   The prospect of the jewel cask
          Might mean he pays you in a trice.

Simplicius:

          Sapiens, your wise advice
          Is based upon a splendid thought:
          Cunning's best with cunning fought!
265   Let's go and put the scheme in motion.
          Sapiens; I have a notion

That, whether we succeed or fail,
We'll take the wind from Lux's sails.

Exeunt. Enter Reichenburger:

If I contrive to keep the loot
270   I'll seek more profit via this route.
A merchant must use cunning tricks
These days, or he'd be in a fix.

Wife:

Husband, I've just had a thought.
Do you think our friend will go to court
275   Or give his money up for lost?

Reichenburger:

I think he will have guessed the cost
Of challenging someone so strong.
He won't stay round here very long.
Who's knocking at the door so late?

Wife:

280   From his clothes and his bald pate,
The merchant who sells gems and jewels.

Reichenburger:

Then let him in! The silly fool
Might want to pawn some precious stones.
I'll bleed him dry and bleach his bones!

Enter the old merchant, bowing:

285   Worthy Sir, noble and pious,
My travels take me soon to Venice.
Nothing here on earth would move me
To take these jewels on my journey.
Twelve thousand sovereigns worth, at least!
290   They need protection from some thief.
My first thought was to come to you,
Known to all as truer than true;
Most suited of the townsfolk here
To keep my hoard of gems secure
295   For three months. I have also heard
You're soon to be host to some Lord!
This I'd dearly like to see.

Reichenburger:
>My house is yours, Sir, please feel free.
>Your stones will be safe in my care.
>300   I've kept things sometimes for a year
>For strangers: often large amounts.
>In these things, reputation counts!

Enter Simplicius:
>Goodly Sir, I have come back
>To take possession of my sack
>305   Of gold, left in your stewardship.

Reichenburger, offering his hand:
>My friend, you've had an arduous trip!
>I thought your lengthy absence meant
>You'd met with some bad accident.
>I feared you never would come back.
>310   Go fetch the gentleman his sack!

Simplicius:
>And what, Sir, is your normal fee?

Reichenburger:
>That really isn't up to me.
>If you wish - some token for my wife.
>She's scrimped and saved up all her life,
>315   Investing every penny piece
>To ensure our nest-egg should increase.

Wife, giving him the sack:
>Here's your sack: the seal's intact.
>There's nothing missing, that's a fact!

Simplicius:
>Thank you. And may I now offer
>320   These two sovereigns for your coffer.

Exit Simplicius with his sack. The merchant, giving the wife a ring:
>Dear Lady, please accept this ring
>As token of the finer things
>To come, when I retrieve my wares.

Wife:
>The Lord look after your affairs!

124

The merchant:
>   325   Adieu, kind Sir, I must depart.

Exit. Reichenburger:
>   The Lord embrace you to his heart
>   And speed you on your southward way!

Wife:
>   I wish a thunderbolt would slay
>   Him. We've just lost a king's own ransom!

Reichenburger:
>   330   This box might just prove twice as handsome.
>   We couldn't have refused the other,
>   Or this one might have run for cover,
>   Fearing I might cheat him too.
>   This time the booty won't slip through
>   335   Our fingers: we will keep the lot!

Wife:
>   Let's have a look at what we've got.
>   Pretty jewels and noble gems,
>   Rings, and charms, and diadems!
>   And if you need to cover your tracks,
>   340   You can always repair the seal with wax.

Reichenburger, breaking the seal and peering into the little casket:
>   Damn and blast it! That old devil
>   Has fooled us with a load of gravel
>   And some old straw! This world is full
>   Of treachery and types who'll pull
>   345   Off dirty tricks! Why, just last week
>   A tenant had the downright cheek
>   To steal from me; and then, next day,
>   Some thief took my best carp away
>   From the tank where they are kept and fed.
>   350   I'll soon be wishing I was dead
>   If our bad luck can't be turned around.

Wife, showing him the ring:
>   This ring is made of glass, confound
>   It! That old rogue has fooled and cheated
>   Us. We'll be humiliated.
>   355   Merchantmen, like vagabonds,
>   Are not to be relied upon!

And we thought we were crafty sinners!
Come on, let's go and eat our dinner.

Exeunt. Enter Sapiens and Simplicius. Simplicius:

            My grateful thanks, good Sapiens,
360   Your wisdom's helped me make amends.
            You've saved me from a wretched mess.
            When next you see your friend, please stress
            My never-ending gratitude.
            In future, I shall be more shrewd,
365   Investing where my money earns
            A profit, and will be returned!

Sapiens closes the play:

            When I see him I'll convey
            Your thanks. You've had a chance today
            To learn a lesson: only trade
370   With men to whom respect is paid
            By all; whose upright reputation
            Is based on trust and sound relations
            With their honest, pious friends.
            Above all, go to any ends
375   To circumvent those steeped in greed,
            Whose lust for money only leads
            To avarice and vile dishonour.
            They risk their reputation on a
            Quest for ever greater wealth -
380   Would sell their mortal soul itself,
            If it would fetch the proper price.
            What they have cannot suffice:
            They scrimp and save from dawn to dusk,
            Slaves to their own venal lust.
385   'Greed makes a rod for honest backs:
            God save us from it' says Hans Sachs.

Dramatis personae:

Lux Reichenburger, an avaricious man
Simplicius, a guileless man
Sapiens, a wise man
The old jewel merchant
Maria, Reichenburger's wife.
            Anno 1551, on the 5th day of September.

5. *The Adulterers' Bridge*, 1530.

9. THE RED-HOT POKER

Ein faßnachtspil mit 3 person
Das heiß eysen
16 November 1551

As is the case with *The Crying Pup, Evil Fumes,* and *The Travelling Scholar in Paradise,* the main themes in this play are those of marital strife, mutual trust, or a lack of it, fidelity, and reconciliation, or the lack of it. Here, in the shortest of the plays in this selection, the wife suspects that the cooling of the relationship between her and her husband, four years into their marriage, is a sign that he is seeking comfort in the arms of other women. Her plight is such as to elicit the sympathy of the audience, and she seeks, not unnaturally, the advice of an older relative ('Gevatterin', which would normally mean 'godmother', 'friend', 'neighbour', or 'female relative', is rendered in this translation as 'cousin', which has appropriate period connotations in the English). The cousin's advice, allegedly rooted in folk tradition, seems not unreasonable: the husband should have his faithfulness put to the test. The drastic nature of the test - picking up a red-hot poker and proving one's innocence by not being burned - smacks of the most drastic 'ducking stool justice' and promises some highly entertaining physical comedy.

The wife's casual aside that her husband will have no chance if the two women conspire, particularly since she has always been able to fool him with her well-rehearsed false sighs and tears, gives the audience a fair idea of how the drama will develop: as is the case with *The Travelling Scholar in Paradise*, the wife is by no means the injured innocent she might at first appear, although she is by no means as malevolent as the wife in *Evil Fumes*.

The husband's quite justifiable protest that he is too tired and worried to be able to display much affection, no doubt expresses a sentiment familiar to sixteenth- and twentieth-century audiences alike. He grudgingly agrees to the test by fire, but is worried by his wife's erratic behaviour: not too worried, though, to play a trick on her and to ensure he passes the test by slipping a piece of wood up his sleeve to protect his flesh. The splendid ritual commences: the test is passed, albeit by cheating. But the husband now reacts in a manner typical of the world of Sachs's carnival comedies. Sauce for the goose is sauce for the gander, and the husband insists that his wife's probity be tested. Her panic-stricken series of confessions, each one worse than the last - her claim that she had only seven lovers, and only intermittently, is revealed as excluding the town bachelors - leaves us with a radically altered perception of an apparently mistreated wife. She who voiced doubts about her husband's fidelity has had numerous lovers. She it is, then, who is burnt by the poker, having instigated the entire matter.

It is the cousin who plays the vital mediating role: for this Sachs play will not end in unresolved recriminations and bitterness, and in this respect it differs considerably from *Evil Fumes*. The cousin's appeal: 'who has not sinned?' (line 240) is answered by the husband's belated confession that he too has indeed strayed from the path of marital fidelity (lines 244-45). A reconciliation is effected - or at least there is the promise of reconciliation. All is clearly not well between the husband and wife, and his agreement with the cousin, that she will, in future, effectively spy on his wife to ensure that she does not stray, is hardly a recipe for a long and trusting relationship. But for the immediate future there will be no more such barbaric tests of faith, and the fabric of the marriage, although apparently rather flimsy, will not be subjected to such a potentially destructive test again.

The Red-Hot Poker

Enter the wife:

> Our marriage is just four years old,
> And my husband's love grown all but cold.
> The flame in my heart's almost spent -
> This state of things was never meant.
> 5   I wonder where the fault may lie?
> But wait - my cousin's passing by!
> She's old and wise, and probably
> Can help me solve the mystery
> Of why my fortunes are so low.
> 10   I'd sleep at night if I could know.

The old cousin:

> Talking to yourself, my dear?

Wife:

> I'm troubled, cousin, as you'll hear.
> I think my man has broken his vow
> And plays with other women now.
> 15   I need your wisdom and advice.

Cousin:

> That accusation's none too nice.

Wife:

> Then tell me how to seek the truth.

Cousin:

> When I was not so long in the tooth,
> We had a custom, tried and tested,
> 20   That if a man should be requested
> To prove his innocence, then we
> Would form a circle, and, with glee,
> Place a red-hot poker in his hand.
> Those free of guilt received no brand:
> 25   The searing heat left not a trace,
> And innocence had proved its case.
> So get to work, arrange the test;
> Your man should come at your behest
> And face the dread ordeal by fire!

Wife:

30   He'll have no chance if we conspire!
I'll fool him with false sighs and tears,
An art I've learnt these past four years,
And he'll soon follow like a lamb.

Cousin:

Take good care now with our plan.
35   Make him fall into the trap
And he'll soon wear the dunce's cap!
Hush! Your husband's coming near.
I'll hide myself. You bend his ear.

Exit cousin. The wife sits, head in hands. Enter husband:
Hello, dear wife, you're looking sad!

Wife:

40   Oh husband, things are truly bad.
I have a sadness in my heart
Which none can cure, with skill or art,
Unless that man be you, my dear.

Husband:

If that is true, then let me hear
45   How I may help in any way.

Wife:

Husband, dear, I have to say
I feel the fault does lie with you:
Your love for me is no longer true.
You lust for others, not your wife.

Husband:

50   Falsely spoken, on my life!
What evidence have you of this?

Wife:

My word are true, I must insist!
You are a stranger to me now
A stranger, too, to your wedding vows.
55   My love for you can't help but wane
When treated with such clear disdain.
Fornication has its price!

Husband:

Your lack of patience is a vice!
My love is rooted good and deep,
60   But daily chores and worries sweep
The joy and brightness from my life;
And now I hear from my own wife
I'm false, when I'm a pious man.

Wife:

You fornicate just like a ram!
65   Sweet innocence you may pretend,
But I'll see you punished in the end.

Husband raises two fingers:

I'll swear to you upon my life
I've not betrayed you once, dear wife,
With other pretty maidens fair.

Wife:

70   Your oaths, dear man, are just hot air,
And sworn as one might shell new peas.

Husband:

Is there no way, wife, that I can please?

Wife:

Yes! Take the red-hot poker test
And prove your innocence to the rest!

Husband:

75   I'll do it, wife, and right away.
Go tell your cousin, without delay,
To heat the iron glowing hot.
I'll take your test, and prove I'm not
Untrue - and then, upon my life,
80   I'll satisfy both cousin and wife.

Exit wife. Husband continues:

My poor wife's mind has gone astray:
She plagues me with a strange array
Of moods - and now this test of fire,
To show the village I'm no liar
85   And that my marriage is intact.
She worries me, and that's a fact.
I've never queried her good name,

Assuming she'd behave the same.
Well, now I'll play a little prank,
90   And up my sleeve put this section of plank:
When it's time to take the test
I'll slide it down and let it rest,
Unseen, upon my wrist and palm:
And then the heat will do no harm.
95   When my virtue passes this ordeal,
We'll see just how the others feel.

Enter old cousin, carrying the poker in a pair of pincers:

Scratch a circle in the earth,
And let us see what you are worth.
Carry the poker if you dare,
100   Then we'll learn if you're foul or fair.
Give your wife what she requires -
Proof your faith can withstand fire.

Husband:

There! The circle's nice and wide.
Lay the poker down inside:
105   Prop it up against this chair.
If the accusation's fair
And I'm untrue and prone to sin -
Well, then the heat will scorch my skin.

Husband carries poker out of circle:

Here's assurance for you, wife!
110   I've not betrayed you, on my life.
I've kept our marriage vows intact -
The red-hot poker proves the fact.
It's left no mark nor brand of shame!

Wife:

Just let me see that hand again!

Husband:

115   The right hand is the one I used.
You'll see that is not even bruised.

Wife looks at hand:

You're right, your hand's not even red.
I must take back all that I've said.

Husband:

Yes. Now I've proved my constancy,
120   You will retract this calumny.

Wife:

For now we'll let the matter rest
And speak no more of faith, or tests.

Husband:

No doubt you've seen enough for now -
But can you make the self-same vow,
125   And swear to me that you've not faltered
Since the day we left the altar?
Cousin! Play your part again;
Take the poker, tell me when
It glows and sizzles with the heat -
130   We'll re-enact this little treat
And test my dear wife's probity,
To see if she's been true to me!

Cousin:

O come now! Leave your wife in peace.
This poker test should surely cease.

Husband:

135   She's the one who started this!

Wife:

But husband, dear, don't take amiss
My simple fears you were a knave.

Husband:

Your pleading, dearest, cannot save
You from the test. Go stoke the fire!

Cousin exits with poker. Wife:

140   But husband, you must still your ire.
I love you more than tests can prove.

Husband:

Your deeds betray your shallow love.
You forced me into this ordeal.

Wife:

Oh husband, please think how I feel.

145 Trust me, I am yours for life:
You'll never find a truer wife.
Let us cease this silly game.

Husband:

Wife, there's no need to complain.
If you've kept faith, there'll be no harm
150 Nor pain to either hand or arm.
Your wifely virtue will be plain.
So plead no more - you've much to gain.

Cousin, bringing the red-hot poker, putting it on the chair in the circle:

The poker waits upon the chair -
Prove your innocence if you dare!

Husband:
155 Well, go on! Get a good strong hold!

Wife:

Relent, I beg, and I'll unfold
The tale of my adultery:
For many times I have made free
With the chaplain, in a secret place.
160 Forgive me just this one disgrace
And leave my hand and arm unburnt!

Husband:

What's this? You tell me now you weren't
Faithful to me these four years?
Take the poker - disappear -
165 And take the cursed chaplain, too!

Wife:

Oh husband, dear, I've not been true.
Can you find it in your heart, perhaps,
To overlook another lapse
Or two, I really must confess?

Husband:
170 No wonder that your love grew less,
Since there were three men you preferred.
Your claim to love me is absurd:
You who seemed so chaste and pure
And made me take this test of fire.

175   I'll ignore your infidelity,
        If the poker test convinces me!

Wife holds up her hands:
        Oh husband, dear, another plea:
        I've hoarded money secretly.
        Four golden sovereigns I have saved,
180   By doing without the food I craved.
        This treasure's yours - if you'll forget
        Four other lovers I have met.
        Say yes and I will take the test!

Husband:
        You slut! You surely speak in jest.
185   You've brought disgrace on all your kin,
        And seem to think it no great sin
        To betray me with so many men!

Wife:
        Only seven - and now and then!

Husband:
        It might as well have been a score!
190   But once again, the iron can draw
        The truth from you. I've said my piece;
        Just take the test, and we shall cease
        To think of your iniquity.

Wife:
        If only it could set me free!
195   But wait - the seven we've noted down
        Exclude the bachelors from the town!
        I'll take no test if they're involved!

Husband:
        Shut up! This case will soon be solved.
        Carry the iron while it's hot
200   From the ring, and then I'll not
        Have cause for any doubts or fears -
        I'll know what I've had these last four years.

Wife:
        O cousin, carry it for me, please!

Cousin:

205

Oh no, my girl! If I should seize
The iron it would scorch and burn:
My skin and hair would surely turn
Quite black - it's years since I've been chaste!

Husband:

210

Enough of this! Don't try to waste
My time, you low and faithless whore!
If you delay things any more,
You'll feel my fist, and no mistake!

Wife:

The iron's still glowing, but I must take
The risk: it seems I have no choice.
In this respect I have no voice.

The wife picks up the poker, sets off, screams, drops it:

215

Jesus Christ! my skin's on fire!
The test has proven I'm a liar
And branded me for all to see!

Husband:

220

That's your reward for doubting me,
You slut. Considering your role,
You've got off lightly, on the whole.
I've every right to tan your hide!

Wife:

Not with my brothers by my side!

Cousin:

225

O cousin think! and hold your tongue.
The game is lost, your husband's won.
The tricks you played on him were foul -
You have no right to pout and scowl.
Work to mend your wicked ways,
Or else the bogeyman will flay
Your hide, and punish your excess!

Exit wife. Husband:

230

My wife thought me a fool, I guess -
Pretending she was pure and chaste,
Respectable, and quite straight-laced.
She tried to force me to obey

Her whims, and prove I hadn't strayed.
235 But jealousy and faithlessness
Combined ensured she failed the test.
Her honour's gone, her guilt's revealed.

Cousin:

O cousin, let this wound be healed.
Forgive your sinner of a wife:
240 For who has not sinned in this life?
Come, let us sit and drink a toast.

Husband:

She is forgiven - for I can't boast
That I have never left the path
Of virtue, nor betrayed my hearth
245 And home. But only on condition you
Will guarantee that she'll be true,
By keeping watch on her for me.

Cousin:

Oh cousin, dear, assuredly!
Come, let's all go back to your house.
250 And, when we're there we will carouse,
Rekindling love in all our hearts
And celebrating a new start!
'We'll have no more of these attacks
With red-hot pokers', says Hans Sachs.

Dramatis personae:

The Husband
The wife
The cousin

Anno salutis 1551, on the 16th day of November.

10. DIONISIUS THE TYRANT

Faßnachtspiel mit 4 personen. Der tyrann Dionisius
mit Damone seiner glückseligkeit halber
28 January, 1553

In taking as his subject a foreign, historical tyrant, Sachs would
seem, not for the first time in this selection, to be straying from the tried
and tested arena of carnival comedy. Here, he allows himself a degree of
latitude in order to examine the question of the nature of the ruler's lot
and his relationship with his people - particularly a ruler who rides
roughshod over the common man. The play provides evidence of Sachs's
astute political understanding that the 'era of the common man', as it is
popularly known, was no different from any other era: for what Sachs
illustrates here is the old adage that might is right, and that might resides
in the hands of a very few people, and not always legitimately. The play
might well be seen as a precursor of the 'Fürstenschule' ('School for
Princes') dramas of Gryphius, Lohenstein, Hallman, and Anton Ulrich in
the seventeenth century, which hold up a mirror to those destined for
power or already exercising power. Equally, its theme of the servant
playing King for a day is a central motif in Shrovetide and carnival
celebrations.

But much as the play might promise to offer a serious analysis of
the nature of kingship, or of the nature of tyranny, to be more precise, its

true focus remains the human rather than the political, as one would expect of Sachs. What we are shown here is the all-too-fallible, human face of Dionisius, as revealed to Damon in his own turn terrified by the reality of ruling: or rather ruling as portrayed to him by the jaded, disillusioned cynic, Dionisius. The play does offer political insights, but its chief merit is as a study of greed for power on the one hand, and of satiation leading to near disgust on the other, as well as of human folly disguised by absolute authority. Yet the play opens with an immensely powerful recitation by Dionisius of his position and his achievements: conquest, subjugation, absolute command, terror tactics from the iron fist of the tyrant. Dionisius would not seem merely to be playing a reluctant role - he apparently relishes his position. Damon's fawning speech confirms Dionisius's position as that of the all-powerful ruler - if not so much in himself or compared with other major potentates, as Damon claims, then certainly as far as his own court goes. But Sachs rapidly sows the seed of doubt: why, if Dionisius is supremely powerful, does he not enjoy his position? Why does he never laugh? Damon's simple question, coming in the context of a carnival comedy and of Shrovetide itself, is all the more interesting, and allows Dionisius to indulge in a little sport with his councillor, by offering to make him king for the day. Sachs skates over the interlude between this scene and the next, which takes place near dawn, in order to sustain the momentum. But he does afford the audience a penetrating insight into Damon, who cannot sleep a wink at the thought of his imminent 'elevation': even though the terms of the promotion are clear and the whole thing is a quasi-carnival game, Damon allows himself to confuse theatre and reality to such an extent that he dreams of actually being promoted to viceroy in Sicily. Folly indeed! His nascent delusions of grandeur are nourished by the donning of the purple robes and the *trappings* of kingship, and there emerges at this stage an interestingly Macchiavellian side to Damon: his 'man for all seasons' support for

Dionisius, and the self-serving nature of his loyalty (line 80 ff.) But now a little play within a play commences - itself not an unusual feature of Sachs's carnival comedies, as we have seen elsewhere in this selection. [1] The guards Dion and Nisius, who, as their names suggest, are veritably the creatures of Dionisius, prepare to enact their mime of the dangers facing the tyrant from those who are nearest to him. The 'little show' is designed by Dionisius to frighten Damon (line 95). Dion and Nisius also have the genuine clarity of vision of those close to the tyrant but whose great ambition is to be successful in protecting their ruler and thus to survive without incurring his wrath - unlike Damon, who has succumbed to ambition.

Damon now begins to evince the well-known syndrome of absolute authority corrupting absolutely (line 135). Unlike the *mock* kings of Shrovetide and other carnival festivals, Damon has managed to blur the line between reality and fantasy and has become a *fake* king. Faced now with the apparently life-threatening insubordination of Dion and Nisius, he lacks any authority and is rapidly brought to a state of sobriety and bitter disillusionment, recognising that even a king's life hangs by a thread and that even a mighty potentate is never truly safe from harm. Dionisius mockingly expresses wonderment and concern at this sudden sea-change, and goes on to underline the grim, precarious nature of his own existence. Damon, rid of his own delusions, now comes back to addressing the question of Dionisius's position: loyalty cannot be expected from those being choked by the iron fist, envy and hatred are ignored at the tyrant's peril, friends and courtiers are equally untrustworthy. History supplies its lessons in the form of the Greeks and Carthaginians. Indeed, at this juncture, Sachs gives Dionisius some of the strongest rhetorical writing to be found in any of his carnival comedies - a genre generally given to plain

---

[1] See Chapter 8, footnote two, p. 112.

speech. Dionisius's vision of the future crumbling of his now mighty position, with its repetitions of 'then', 'then', (lines 255 ff.) is truly impressive. And not even the Gods will help: Dionisius has only paid contemptuous lip-service to them over the years, and they will surely exact their revenge for that. Small wonder, then, that Dionisius is a sombre melancholic, harbouring as he does this vision within him of the real world of absolute tyrannical authority.

What, then, is Sachs telling his audience here? That their rulers are only human? That power does not bring happiness? That kings and tyrants who are corrupt will suffer a wretched fate in due course? These might have been the lessons to be drawn from the likes of Gryphius, or Anton Ulrich, had they used this material. Sachs, it seems, emphasises more than anything else in this play that Damon's ambitions are false and inappropriate. He should settle for serving in the ranks, and not aspire to emulate the great Dionisius, whose position is, in any case, not as enviable as it might seem. Sachs, not surprisingly, is not advocating republicanism; he certainly criticises Dionisius, but not the institution of kingship, and not individual kings if they rule in a decent manner. Tyrants are a different matter, and it is the personal weakness, the urge towards despotic behaviour, the insecurity resulting from tyranny, which are highlighted by Sachs. He is, as one might expect, expressing a conservative ideal: of humane, god-fearing rulers being served by those who know their place as loyal subjects. The alarming vision of Dionisius's court and the nature of his misrule are meant to act as negatively didactic agents - like Lear, or Macbeth in other, grander contexts.

Dionisius the Tyrant.
In which Dionisius discusses happiness with Damon.

Enter Dionisius, the tyrant, with Damon, a councillor, and two guards:

         The mighty realm of Sicily
         Is conquered, and upon his knees
         The former King is forced to bow,
         Accepting I'm his master now.
5   On his back he'll wear my yoke.
         My bit and bridle act as tokens
         Of my absolute command.
         I'll keep control throughout the land
         With the iron fist of tyranny,
10   And treat dissenters viciously.
         My throne's set up in Syracuse,
         From where I shall, if Fortune chooses,
         Rule by fear and naked power.

Damon, his councillor:

         This ranks among your finest hours,
15   Majesty. The world's not seen
         A greater ruler. There's not been
         Your equal in the Hall of Kings
         For dominating underlings.
         No oriental potentate
20   Could ever hope to subjugate
         His peoples in the way you do.
         Forgive me, but I can't construe
         Why you should never seem content,
         And why it seems your life is spent
25   In sadness. You have never once
         Been seen to laugh, as evidence
         Of your enjoyment. In your place,
         I'm sure a smile might cross my face
         When I considered my position.

Dionisius:

30   To understand a king's condition
         You must have experience.
         If you desire, I'll let you sense
         Some of the joys of being king,

Some of the comforts ruling brings.
35   Tomorrow you shall start, at dawn.

Damon:

But how can I, a humble pawn,
Deserve such graciousness, O Sire?
One who never could aspire
To know the bliss of regal station?

Dionisius:
40   For now, let our sole occupation
Be dining. Soon you'll be exposed
To all the bliss a king can know.

Exeunt. Enter Damon:

I haven't slept a wink tonight,
Thinking of the awesome height
45   To which this royal act of grace
Will elevate a man so base.
What joys there are for me to relish!
The King himself may well embellish
Me with a title: he may install
50   Me as Viceroy over all
This glorious isle of Sicily,
To govern by direct decree,
Establishing his right to reign
In all the isle, as he may deign.
55   Before this very day is out
The issue will be beyond doubt.

Enter Dion, the guard:

Damon, royal councillor,
His Majesty would now confer
With you, and bids you not to waste
60   A moment, but to make all haste
To join him - then to take his throne,
To bear the sceptre and don the crown.
You're to wear his finery,
His ornaments and jewellery,
65   And his royal purple raiment.
Then begins the entertainment -
As you feel the joys and woes
That every reigning monarch knows.

Exit Dion. Damon:

I face the future confident
70   The King will prove munificent:
Bestowing on me royal favours
From a heart that's learnt to savour
All my faith and loyalty.
Throughout his years of tyranny,
75   No matter how unjust his actions,
He's always had the satisfaction
Of my support, as I pretend
His means are sanctioned by his ends.
I am the King's most loyal servant:
80   And most deserving of preferment.

Exit. Enter the two guards. Nisius:

What can Dionisius have in mind,
That we two guards should stand behind
The royal throne, as Damon takes
His place, and that we two should fake
85   An attitude of ill-intent,
As if we are on murder bent?
I'm to feign a fierce attack,
And aim my arrow at his back,
While you approach him stealthily,
90   Raising your great sword, so he
Will think you mean to run him through.

Dion:

I find I'm puzzled, just like you.
Perhaps he means this little show
To frighten Damon, so he'll know
95   The real nature of his master:
A tyrant, whose wrath spells disaster
For anyone who vexes him,
Friend or foe, kith or kin.
The King's an evil and capricious
100   Monster, who dispenses vicious
Pain and torment, on a whim.
Only one thing interests him:
How to subjugate through fear.

Nisius:

There's none quite like him, far or near:
105   A king as harsh as he's unfair,
Who makes it plain he doesn't care

A fig for gods or mortal men.
We pray he dies to put an end
To his monstrous ways, his tyrant's thirst
110   For blood. His rule's become the worst
Example of sustained disquiet -
And such has been our daily diet.

Dion:

Though we're among the least affected.
Come: our new King's to be protected.

Exeunt. Enter Dionisius in simple clothing and Damon in regal garb. Dionisius:

115   Damon, sit down on my throne.
Today this seat is yours alone.
Dispose of things at your discretion:
Make full use of your royal position.
Your lackeys and your guards surround
120   You; councillors whose views you'll sound
Out; and your chancellor attends;
Your courtiers, and all your friends;
Your actors, fit for comedy
Or some appalling tragedy;
125   Your tumblers and your acrobats;
And those who wrestle on the mat;
Your swordsmen, and your graceful fencers;
Everything to please the senses
Of a temporary King.
130   You'll not lack a single thing
To help you feel the true delight
A king can savour, day or night.

Damon, sitting down:

My heart is truly overflowing,
Given now the chance of knowing
135   Absolute authority:
The essence of serenity.
Today, just on this one occasion,
I control and steer the nation.
And if tomorrow I should die,
140   I'll not depart this world with sighs.
The memory of rank and power
Will sweeten even my dying hour.

Enter the two guards, Dion and Nisius, one bearing a bow, the other a two-edged sword. Both adopt an attitude of attack. Damon:

> You dare submit me to attack?

Nisius:

> Hold your tongue, or you'll soon lack
> 145   The breath to play your royal part.
> This arrow's aimed right at your heart -
> And if I choose to let it fly
> You'll split in two and then you'll die.
> Your life's entirely in my hands.

Damon:

> 150   Desist! Obey your King's commands!
> Do you not know that for today
> Damon's every word holds sway?
> Desist! Or you'll be put to death!

Dion:

> You may as well save your breath.
> 155   We're staying here in our positions.
> And I'll add just one more condition:
> If you don't take back what you said,
> This sword will easily split your head.

Damon, looking up, seeing the unsheathed sword suspended over his head:

> Ah! Now I truly recognise
> 160   The peril right before my eyes.
> A mighty sword which seems suspended
> By a breath, and poised to end
> My wretched life with just one blow.
> The power and glory, fresh bestowed
> 165   On me, have turned to bitter gall.
> Once more I'm at your beck and call,
> Dionisius. Please resume your throne.
> Release me, and while you alone
> Shall rule, allow me to pursue
> 170   The humbler path of serving you.
> My lust for power has disappeared.

Dionisius:

> That's strange music to my ears,
> Damon. Have you not been granted
> Every privilege you wanted?
175 > Have you not, then, shared my bliss?
> Are you not content with this?
> Now you're steeped in royal matters,
> Why can you not laugh and chatter?
> Why do you seem so dismayed?

Damon:

180 > Any sense of joy has faded
> Now I've seen reality.
> A sharp sword hanging over me;
> Grim-faced guards behind my back,
> Always ready to attack
185 > Me, hastening me to early death.
> When I sit with bated breath,
> How can I enjoy my reign?

Dionisius:

> My situation's just the same,
> Dear Damon. I am equally
190 > Surrounded. I am never free:
> Constantly exposed to danger,
> Prey to any friend or stranger.

Damon:

> But you can bask in all your glory!
> Yours is quite a different story.
195 > Your complaint is meant in jest!

Dionisius:

> If you could put me to the test,
> You'd find my heart so malcontent
> It has lost the power to lament.
> Beneath this show of regal splendour,
200 > Awful terrors are engendered.
> Outwardly I'm unperturbed,
> Appearances remain superb -
> The purple garb and royal crown -
> But, underneath it all, I'm bound,
205 > No matter what the circumstance,
> To keep eternal vigilance.

My life is grim. Now you know why.
The joys of kings are circumscribed.

Damon:

      How can that be true? You rule
210 A mighty empire, with every tool
      Of government made to ensure
      Your subjects fear you all the more.
      You have no fear of enemies here.

Dionisius:

      You're right. My subjects go in fear.
215 But I have learnt to fear them all.
      Their hearts are full of bitter gall.
      They may pretend that they are loyal,
      But, secretly, the yearn to foil
      Me. I can draw no comfort there.

Damon:

220 But surely, Sire, the people care
      For you - they're not your enemy?

Dionisius:

      They hate me for my tyranny.
      For years, I've exercised a grip
      Of iron, and my stewardship
225 Has placed on them a vexing yoke.
      I squeeze them so hard that they choke.
      Is their loyalty to be expected?
      They'd kill me if I weren't protected.
      I live in fear of mutiny
230 Designed to set the people free.
      I've given them sufficient grounds
      And wonder why they haven't found
      A way of poisoning my food,
      Or stabbing me. And hence this mood.

Damon:

235 But you're surrounded by your friends!
      Your guards and lackeys all defend
      You. How and where are you exposed?

Dionisius:

>Damon, everybody knows
>That many kings in many lands
240 Have perished at their own guards' hands.
>I never draw an easy breath.

Damon:

>You've never even courted death
>In war! Good fortune's always stood
>Beside you, and you have a good
245 And loyal band of friends. Rejoice!

Dionisius:

>I wouldn't dare to raise my voice.
>My life's the same in war and peace.
>Victories no doubt increase
>My power, but my enemies
250 Grow stronger and won't be appeased.
>The Greeks and Carthaginians
>Were toppled by their minions.
>Why should fortune show me favour?
>Now a strong man, I'll soon quaver.
255 Then I'll flee the battlefield;
>Then I'll see my soldiers yield;
>Then I'll hunger for provisions;
>Then I'll want for ammunition;
>Then my allies will defect;
260 Then I'll forfeit all respect;
>Then I'll truly be exposed.
>Fortune, strongest of man's foes,
>Plays with me like a balloon:
>Floating now, but all too soon
265 To be deflated. I must wait
>To see the nature of my fate.
>Who will tell me, friend or foe?
>Will I die slow enough to know?
>Feeling this, can I rejoice?

Damon:
270 But Sire, you make your sacrifice
>Every day, and say your prayers.
>This should alleviate your cares -
>Knowing that the gods defend
>You from those who seek to end
275 Your life. You have no need to mourn.

Dionisius:

The gods view me with hate and scorn.
I've long since forfeited their favour.
Considering my past behaviour,
They will have no hesitation
280   In meting out full retribution.

Damon:

Yet still you offer them devotions?

Dionisius:

I'm only going through the motions.
You understand, it's all for show.
In my heart of hearts I know,
285   As they do, it is just pretence.

Damon:

But tell me, how is it you sense
The malice that you've just described?

Dionisius:

How could they now be on my side
When I've despised them all these years?
290   When all along I've laughed and jeered
At them, defacing all their shrines?
When I never once have felt inclined
To keep an oath sworn in their name?
I've played the same disloyal games
295   With men and gods indifferently.
And hence the mournful face you see.
When there's no room in someone's heart
For joy and happiness, he starts
To lapse into a sombre state.
300   Surrounded, as I am, by hate
And fear, of which you've had a taste,
My life's become a tedious waste
Of time and effort. What you thought
Was bliss, is nothing of the sort.
305   And now you wish to be released?

Damon:

Without the least regret, I'll cease
My reign, return your robes and crown,

Lay the royal sceptre down,
And with a sigh of grateful thanks
310   Return to serving in the ranks.
I shall not again aspire
To emulate your greatness, Sire.

'Kings must always fear attacks
From every quarter', says Hans Sachs.

Dramatis personae:

Dionisius, the tyrant.
Damon, his councillor.
Dion, a guard.
Nisius, a guard.

Anno 1553, on the 28th day of January.

11. THE INQUISITOR AND ALL HIS SOUP CAULDRONS

Faßnacht-spiel mit 5 personen
Der ketzermeister mit den vil kessel suppen
2 October 1553

Here we find Sachs returning to the anti-Catholic territory he had trodden, not without being censured by the civic authorities of Nürnberg, years earlier, when he openly supported Luther and the Reformation in works which might be deemed virulently propagandistic: his *Die wittembergisch nachtigall (1523)*, and the *Disputation zwischen einem chorherrn und schuchmacher (1524)*. [1]

Here, though, the more strident tone of the earlier works is replaced by comedy, but comedy which is nonetheless cruel in its exposure of the nature of the Roman church's servants, and of their attitude, and the church's, towards the common man, of the greed of Catholicism and its servants for earthly goods, and of their hypocrisy in matters of charity and tolerance.

Herman, the Inquisitor's spy, and Simon, the innkeeper, are rapidly characterised in the opening scene: Herman as sly, impecunious, and ready to cheat his neighbour, and Simon as wealthy, but simple to the point of stupidity. Their opening exchanges are apparently friendly, and conducted in an appropriately colloquial tone, as plans are made to have a fine

---

[1] See Chapter Two - *Hans Sachs: Literature to the Last.*

evening, involving eating, cards and dice, and trying out the new Alsatian wine fit to blow off God's socks. This is precisely the sort of evening Sachs's carnival audience would wish to have stretching before it. Such is the superficial amiability of the untrustworthy Herman that the subsequent revelation that he spies for the Inquisitor, and believes he has just ensnared a heretic in the shape of his 'friend' Simon, comes as a shock. The shock is not ameliorated by the grandiose appearance of, and the splendidly self-important, grandiloquent speech of Doctor Romanus: 'as Inquisitor I'm sent to spy by Mother Church on heresy' (lines 45-46). The Inquisitor's motive is clear: to make a financial profit from threatening the common man with eternal damnation for his sins, be they real or not. That his income is falling is alluded to. But why that should be the case - whether the common man is less and less impressed thanks to the influence of Lutheranism, or whether the Inquisitor is losing his touch - remains for the audience to find out.

Herman's report of a nice wealthy sinner, simple to boot, seems to promise an easy and profitable prey for the Inquisitor. And this is where the real tension in the play is introduced: can the all-powerful Catholic papal proxy simply dragoon the innkeeper into obedience, and make a fat profit, or will Simon escape his clutches, just as the birds in the wood have escaped Herman all that morning? In a sense the audience already knows the answer: given his long-held views, and given the nature of his earlier publications, Sachs would clearly not now be writing a play about the triumph of Catholic malpractice. The audience can all sit back and enjoy the unfolding plot, in anticipation of a satisfactory dénouement.

As Simon is summoned to the monastery of the barefoot monks, with its meagre display of cold charity in the form of the daily cauldrons of soup made from vegetable detritus, he fears the worst. His fears are promptly confirmed by the nature of the Inquisitor's attack, accusing him of heresy. His friend Claus, whom he has begged to go with him to help ward off confusion and to comfort him, proves himself a clear-headed sceptic, unafraid of the Inquisitor's blustering threats. Indeed, in response to the Inquisitor, Claus adopts a tone of mockery. He pretends he cannot understand all the rhetoric and bombast, being a simple layman, and proceeds to liken the Inquisitor to an ass and a fool. Claus's mock-innocent disrespect turns to open contempt in the course of a short interview. This does not, of course, aid Simon's cause, as the Inquisitor turns on him with a renewed wrath, threatening excommunication, trial by ducking, or a compulsory pilgrimage.

Simon, though, being a businessman, is mightily heartened when Claus tells him that the hooded vulture merely wants the right amount of money, and is not interested in metaphysical matters. The mystique of the Catholic Church is torn away, and in the ensuing interview between inquisitor and would-be victim, it is Simon, heartened by his new-found insight, who will gain the upper hand, simply by refusing to be cowed by the previously intimidating mumbo-jumbo of the Inquisitor. Having paid attention during the sermon through which he was forced to sit, he turns the tables on his foe, in the same way as Luther used to when confronted by Catholic scholars, by applying a Biblical analogy to real life. The thousands of gallons of soup dispensed by the monastery will, according to the Bible, be returned a hundredfold: and Simon develops a surreal and gruesome image of the monks drowning with bulging eyes in this sea of reciprocated charity.

The Inquisitor is left to swallow a bitter pill - being humbled by 'the common man', being exposed as a hypocrite, and being treated with utter contempt. His fears for the very survival of the Catholic Church, which he and others like him strive to prop up, are met by Sachs's cursory verdict that the institution is close to ruin for the reasons outlined in the play: its servants are decadent, and given to corrupt practices.

A play, then, to warm the cockles of the Lutheran heart.

The Inquisitor and All his Soup Cauldrons

Enter Herman Pich:

I don't know what I've got to do
To try and catch a bird or two;
I've wandered round the woods and back,
But still there's nothing in my sack,

5   And back at home the cupboard's bare.
But wait! That's Simple Simon there:
He's rich as pigshit - twice as thick -
With all the sense of half a brick.
I've pulled his leg a thousand times,

10   And lost count of just how much wine
I've tricked him out of at his inn.
Let's find out where our landlord's been.
Perhaps he's been to fetch more wine?
Hey! Simon! Is it opening time?

Enter Simon Wirdt, the innkeeper:

15   I'm off to town to buy some hay,
And oats and straw, so my guests can lay
Their heads on something soft tonight.
I'm trying out a brand new white:
That spicy new Alsatian wine.

20   They say it really tastes divine -
But I needn't touch a drop to know
The stuff is strong enough to blow
The socks off God and John the Baptist,
And to grace the celestial winelist.

25   So if it makes the Good Lord tight,
Imagine how we'll feel tonight!
Come along and bring a mate!

Herman:

Have no fear, we won't be late!
And just in case we're in the mood,

30   Rustle up a bit of food,
And get out all the cards and dice!

Simon:

I'll have it ready in a trice.
But first I've got to get my hay.
I'll see you later on today!

Herman:

> 35 You bet your life we'll meet quite soon -
> But you'll be singing a different tune.
> Your tongue has just let slip a thought
> That, once reported, really ought
> To earn me a nice big reward:
> 40 Almost as fat as is our Lord
> Inquisitor, for whom I work.
> The monastery is where he lurks,
> And where I'll give him my good news:
> A heretic for his thumbscrews!

Exit Herman. Enter Doctor Romanus, the Inquisitor:

> 45 As Inquisitor I'm sent to spy
> By Mother Church on heresy.
> My job: to make a careful list
> Of misbelievers and the gist
> Of what they do and what they say,
> 50 Be it near or far away,
> And whosoever they may be.
> I represent the Papacy.
> I punish those I can enmesh,
> I string them up, or singe their flesh;
> 55 Imprison them from time to time -
> Or, failing that, impose a fine.
> I have but one consistent plan:
> To scare to death the common man.
> Through wily tricks and imprecations,
> 60 I harvest many small 'donations'
> To try and see my coffers filled.
> But, though I've kept my patch well tilled,
> My income these past years has dropped.
> The flow of 'gifts' has almost stopped,
> 65 Despite the efforts of my spies,
> Who act here as my ears and eyes
> And promptly bring to my attention
> Cases where my intervention
> Is required, as papal proxy,
> 70 To confound heterodoxy
> And to defend dear Mother Church.
> The end result of such a search?
> An accusation of such power
> The heretic, within the hour,
> 75 Will shit a huge great golden pile
> And thank me with a servile smile

For saving an undeserving soul.
And here comes one who's played his role
As master spy: young Herman Pich.
80   He's done his best to make me rich.
So Herman - what's the news today?

Herman, bowing:

Good Doctor, news of succulent prey.
A nice fat pheasant for you to pluck.

Inquisitor:

A nice fat peasant? We're in luck!

Herman:
85   You've heard of Simon at the inn?
I tell you now - he's steeped in sin!

Inquisitor:

I've never met him. What's he done?

Herman:

I was up this morning with the sun,
And met him walking in the woods.
90   He said he had a wine so good
That John the Baptist, and, what's more,
Our own dear Lord would hit the floor
And belch and fart, and even worse,
Once they had drunk a single glass!
95   He made them out to be like pigs!

Inquisitor:

Oh! Now we're on to something big!
Per deum, he'll not get away.
A wealthy landlord, did you say?
We'll make his wallet feel the strain!

Herman:
100   Oh yes, my Lord, you'd search in vain
For a richer man in this poor town.
Among the landlords he's renowned
For his wealth and for his stock of wine.
But, when it comes to thinking time,
105   He's simple as his face is plain:
A four-year-old has got more brain.
To escape you he's not bright enough.

Inquisitor:

> I'll pluck his feathers, then I'll stuff
> Him. And you'll get your proper share.
> 110   Now lead me to this sinner's lair!

Herman:

> His inn's down Long Street, near the end.

Inquisitor:

> I'll find the house and then I'll send
> My beadle there, without delay,
> To tell him he should make his way
> 115   To me. You'll see: he'll shit a brick,
> As if he's dealing with Old Nick!

Exeunt. Enter Simon:

> Oh my, oh my, oh dear, oh Lord!
> I'm in more trouble than I can afford.
> For goodness sake what can I do?

Enter Claus, his neighbour:

> 120   What on earth's got into you,
> Simon? You're a quivering heap.
> It's not like you to wail and weep.

Simon:

> I'll tell you, Claus, I've had a visit -
> A beadle sent by the Naquisit.
> 125   He told me I should not delay,
> But go to see him straight away!

Claus:

> The Inquisitor? Well, that's no game.
> At least learn how to say his name!

Simon:

> I mean that greedy fat old friar,
> 130   Who sniffs out all the sinners and liars.
> What on earth does he want with me?

Claus:

> The only reason I can see -
> You've let slip thoughts, however brief,
> That must have smacked of misbelief,
> 135   And someone has reported you.

Simon:

As God's my judge, my faith is true -
I've never had an evil thought.
They say this monk's a pompous sort.
He punishes and vexes folk,
140 And lays on them a heavy yoke,
And has done now for many years.
The thought of him fills me with fear:
He'll ask me what I've done and seen,
And make me say things I don't mean.
145 Oh Claus, old friend, please come with me -
You'll get a glass of wine for free:
The spicy new Alsatian white.
I need someone to help me fight
Against a charge of heresy.

Claus:

150 Tell him you've never hurt a flea,
Nor yet on Friday taken meat.
Just tell the truth - the man won't eat
You. There's no need to be afraid.

Simon:

No. I can't do it without aid.
155 I'm no match for a cunning foe.
He'll tie me up in knots, I know.
Oh Claus, dear neighbour, take my part.

Claus:

I'll help you friend, with all my heart.
To the monastery, without delay!
160 Let's see what the barefoot has to say.
It might be something else, of course:
He might just want to borrow your horse
And cart, to take a little ride.

Simon:

In that case, I've got nothing to hide.
165 He's welcome - and I'll charge no fee.
But we'd best make haste - the clock's struck three,
And soon it will be matins time.
I still feel chills run down my spine!

Exeunt. Enter Inquisitor with Sexton:

Time for afternoon devotions,
170   Sexton. Just go through the motions.
Make the monks sound good and pious,
So the people won't decry us.
May our holy, spiritual ways
Lead them to express their praise
175   In cash, to keep our bellies round!
But don't forget that we are bound
By duty to use all our waste,
No matter how bad it may taste:
Turnip tops and cabbage leaves,
180   Potato peelings and old cheese.
From these we feed the weak and poor
Who gather at the convent door
For soup brewed in monastic cauldrons -
They wolf it down like starving children.

Sexton:

185   Have no fear, your Eminence,
The cauldrons - daily evidence
Of our devoted charity -
Are by the door for all to see.
The poor enjoy their meagre fare:
190   But any meat we have to spare
I'll see is served us cold tonight.
The poor must learn to see things right,
And think we give them lousy slops
As poverty has always stopped
195   Us from providing better things!
The contributions that they bring
Should thus grow bigger! But look here -
Simon from the inn draws near.

Inquisitor:

I've had him summoned to this place
200   To interrogate him, face to face,
And establish here, in one short session,
The nature of his indiscretion,
And then persuade him - mortal sinner -
To contribute a nice big dinner
205   While I've got him in my net.
To underline his sense of debt,
Let the organ thunder proudly,
Sing the gaudeamus loudly!

Exit Sexton. Enter Simon:

God be with you, Holy Sir,
210   I've come to do your bidding here.

Inquisitor:

Are you Simon from the inn
Down Long Street? If so, let's begin.

Simon:

That's my name and that's my road!

Inquisitor:

You little pestilential toad!
215   Your mouth's so full of deadly venom
That even our Dear Lord in Heaven
And John the Baptist are abused.
By your own tongue they stand accused
Of being drunkards, steeped in wine,
220   Who stagger home at closing time,
Like you and all your drunken tribe.
You'll pay the price for such a jibe!
You are a misbelieving liar -
I'll see you roast in eternal fire!
225   Your skin will scorch, your soul will blaze,
And there you'll spend a million days
In torment and perpetual pain.

Claus:

God help you, Simon, think again:
Did you say what he just said?

Simon:

230   Well, talking off the top of my head,
I said to Herman Pich this morning
That I'd ordered something warming -
That spicy wine I'm trying tonight.
I only said it had some bite,
235   And if Saint John and our Dear Lord
Took a drop or two on board
It would make them feel quite merry.

Claus:

Well, I should think that isn't very
Sinful - there's no disrespect
240   Or misbelief that I detect.

Your Lordship, there's no need for wrath,
Or talk of burning like a moth!
The Lord's name hasn't been denied -
So try to see the brighter side!

Inquisitor:

245 No doubt you want to see an end
To this enquiry - heretic's friend!
You've heard, I trust, of heterodoxy?

Claus:

Hetty the doxy, the one who's poxy
And drinks with us on Friday nights?
250 Oh yes! I've heard of her all right!

Inquisitor:

I see you're making fun of me!

Claus:

I hope my tongue is not too free:
I've but a simple layman's brain.

Inquisitor:

You heretics are all the same.
255 I'll see to your excommunication!

Claus:

Extra what? Who's the patient?
Can't you speak like what we do?

Inquisitor:

Are you mad that you don't eschew
Playing the fool and making faces
260 In this holiest of places?
Leave these consecrated portals!

Claus:

You, Sir, are a troubled mortal!
There you stand, your head all stubble,
A look in your eyes inviting trouble -
265 All you need is a cap and bells!

Inquisitor:

You cheeky ass, you'll go to Hell!
I've no more time to waste on you.

Claus:

> You're the ass - you know it's true;
> Look at the colour of your robe!

Inquisitor:

> 270   You'd try the patience of even Job,
> You maladjusted little bastard.

Claus:

> With all respect to you, O master,
> You're a man devoid of honour.
> May the plague descend upon a
> 275   Priest who spies upon his flock!
> But don't think I've come here to mock
> You. I'm just full of brandy wine.
> Be good until we meet next time!

Exit Claus. Inquisitor:

> Who was that rogue? What is his name?
> 280   How dare he try to put to shame
> His betters? I'll not stand such cheek.
> I'll make enquiries, then I'll seek
> His master out. Is he your friend?

Simon:

> Dear Father, I would not offend
> 285   You with madmen of that hue.
> He had been drinking - that was true.
> He happened to come in with me.

Inquisitor:

> He'll find me a bad enemy!
> Now let's seal your immediate fate!
> 290   First, we excommunicate,
> Then consign to eternal flames!

Simon:

> Holy Father! In God's name,
> Forgive me my poor sinful action.
> Christ himself gains satisfaction
> 295   If a sinner should repent!

Inquisitor:

> Your fear of pain is evident.
> My will is that you should remain

Here, with the monks, while I obtain
A judgement on your wretched ways
300   From Rome: the Pope himself appraises
Cases of such magnitude,
Where heresy might be construed.
Perhaps he'll dunk you in the Tiber,
Or he'll test your moral fibre
305   With an eastern pilgrimage,
To help pay for your sacrilege.
Now, go and listen to the mass.
Pay close attention - I will ask
You later what you've seen and heard!
310   You're in my clutches, little bird,
And there you'll stay - have no delusions -
Until you gain my absolution.

Exit Inquisitor. Enter Claus:

Tell me, neighbour, how you fared
With that old monk - you look so scared.
315   Are you still in mortal fear?

Simon:

It feels like I've been here for years!
He tricked me, and I got confused.
And then he said that he could use
Papal powers to have me drowned!

Claus:

320   No, no! He doesn't want a pound
Of flesh: these vultures clad in hoods
Just want your money and your goods.
The real price of your heresy
Is what it takes to buy you free!
325   About three dozen crowns, I'd say.

Simon:

I'd pay a hundred right away,
Rather than be drowned or burnt!
Had I known what I've just learnt -
That money can buy liberty -
330   I would have long since paid my fee!
I thought my one chance of salvation
Lay in prayer and mortification.
But look - I've got to go to church:

        The Inquisitor has said he'll search
335   Me out and see if I've paid attention.

Claus:

        Well, don't forget the thing I mentioned.
        Who knows? You might soon be free.

Simon:

        It can't come soon enough for me!
        I've heard of fire and brimstone preachers,
340   But these monks here can surely teach us
        All what pain and torture mean.

Claus:

        Let's both go in; I'm rather keen
        To hear what your monks have to say
        About sacrifice - and spying for pay!

Exeunt. Enter Inquisitor and Sexton:

345   O father - whose munificence
        Stems from a pious innocence -
        Tell me: what did Simon say
        When you denounced his godless ways?
        Have you fleeced him, like you said?

Inquisitor:

350   He claims that he's just weak in the head,
        And says it's all a big mistake.
        He pleaded with me not to take
        So dim a view, and to forgive
        His sins - he even tried to give
355   Me Bible lessons! But though brash,
        He offered neither goods nor cash!
        I need to tighten up his strings,
        And then we'll see what tune he sings!
        He'll howl for freedom at any cost -
360   But here he comes, and looking lost!

Enter Simon. Inquisitor:

        Well, heretic, how was the service?
        Did the sermon make you nervous?

Simon:

        Father, in your holy church
        Something made my whole mind lurch.
365   I've had the most disturbing thought!

Inquisitor:

        If you're assailed with doubt, you ought
        To tell me: I can give instruction.

Simon:

        No father, that's a false deduction.
        This affects me not one whit!

Inquisitor:

370   Well, who said what, then? Out with it!

Simon:

        The preacher said when we're in Heaven
        Our charity and all we've given
        Will be returned a hundredfold.

Inquisitor:

        Indeed, a simple truth he told.
375   Give freely to the Church, my friend,
        And reap a handsome dividend!
        But this should not give you such qualms.

Simon:

        It's not for me that I'm alarmed.
        My worry - if I may make so free -
380   Is for you and all the monastery.

Inquisitor:

        For all the monks? What do you mean?

Simon:

        I witness every day the scene
        When you haul three great cauldrons out
        And feed the poor for miles about
385   With soup. So, in just one short year,
        Your charity amounts to near
        Eleven hundred cauldrons' worth!
        In Heaven, then, there'll be no dearth
        Of soup for you, since you'll receive -
390   And you said the preacher's to be believed -

A hundred times as much to drink!
And that, dear Father, makes me think
That you and all the monks might drown,
Floating in the soup, face down,
395   Eyes a-bulging like dead rabbits,
Dragged down by the monastic habits
In which you were all interred.
That's what makes me feel disturbed
And makes me shed a piteous tear!

Inquisitor:
400   You little toad, get out of here!
You evil snake, you heretic!
What has made your mind so sick?
Anathema shall be your fate
For ridiculing one so great!
405   Leave this church without delay.
If we meet again, I'll see you sway
From the nearest gallows, where you belong!

Simon:
It's no good saying I'm in the wrong!
I'd rather have been at home today,
410   Reading the Bible in my usual way!
There's one thing, though, I'll swear is true -
I see nothing that's of credit to you
In the monastery - just hypocrisy.
Lots of prayers for all to see -
415   But these are cynical pretence.
I'm only glad that I've seen sense!

Exit Simon. The Inquisitor closes:
There we see the common man,
Sexton: odious and damned,
An unrepentant renegade,
420   Defying those he should obey.
Familiarity breeds contempt,
And fuels the fires of such dissent.
Our cunning ruses down the years
Have been exposed - now no-one fears
425   Or trusts us. They all read the Bible!
The roof of our Church now seems liable
To fall in - the keystone's crumbling -
The edifice might soon come tumbling

Down, no matter how we strive
430 To prop it up and keep alive
A faith which suffers harsh attacks.
'It's close to ruin', says Hans Sachs.

Dramatis personae:

Simon Wirdt, a simple man
Claus, his crafty neighbour
The Inquisitor
The sexton of the Benedictine monastery
Herman Pich, who takes alms.

Anno salutis 1553 , on the 2nd day of October.

6.   *The Princes' Dance*, Hans Schäufeleien and others, 1531?

12. THE CRYING PUP

Ein faßnachtspiel mit vier personen
Das weynent hündlein
25 January 1554

In *The Crying Pup*, Sachs presents us with the unedifying spectacle of a loving and faithful wife, Paulina, being tricked into committing adultery. She acts from the noblest sentiments - a desire to save her marriage - but, paradoxically, decides to sacrifice her honour and her virtue in order to preserve her identity and thus her relationship with her husband.

The plot sounds worthy of Boccaccio, but, according to Keller and Goetze, does not appear to derive from him, or any identifiable source. If we are to believe that it is an original creation, it would be doubly remarkable. In itself, it is a splendid little piece; but for Sachs to present a successful attack on a marriage is extraordinary. Elsewhere in his carnival comedies, he is concerned to preserve or repair the fabric of marriages, or to present marital harmony and marital give-and-take as vital social bonding elements, as is the case with *Evil Fumes, The Red-Hot Poker,* and *The Travelling Scholar in Paradise*. Here, in stark contrast to the normal pattern of things, a loving wife is duped, in the absence of her husband, into consenting to make love to a suitor whose only apparent interest in pursuing her is the conquest itself, rather than any meaningful relationship.

At the outset, Sachs introduces what might seem a stock situation for low comedy - the beautiful wife with an ageing husband who declares his intention of being away from the marital home for a lengthy period of time. In the often sexually titillating world of the *Decamerone*, this scenario would be most likely to lead to a long-planned adultery with a lurking young lover. But here the situation is quite the opposite. Paulina expresses tender concern for Philips, as he prepares to set off on a perilous journey to the Holy Land, and raises the question of how her honour can properly be safeguarded in his absence. He has no doubts about her fidelity, nor about her ability to fend off unwelcome attentions. There is an air here of mutual respect, love, and confidence. Philips utters a parting reminder, more in jest than earnest, one senses, that his wife should not trust chronic deceivers of the sort represented by travelling showmen or cunning old women. With this, Sachs gives a clear hint to the audience of what is to come; but the warning is not taken too seriously by Paulina, who determines to spend the period of her husband's absence withdrawn from society at large and praying for his safe return. To this end, she joins the bishop at prayers.

The seamless transition to the next scene (as Paulina exits, she is being watched by Felix) suddenly introduces the audience to a different atmosphere. Felix's cynical calculation - that the absence of Philips in the Holy Land will allow him time and space to pursue his conquest of Paulina - highlights the would-be lover's lack of respect for the institution of marriage and for the deep mutual love between Paulina and Philips. For Felix, pursuit is a game, conquest the prize; he is rapidly portrayed as shallow and selfish.

Felix makes a nuisance of himself with gifts and serenading, but at this stage of the developing story there is little sense that Paulina will succumb: and Sachs even has her servants portrayed as loyally protective. An interesting comparison may be drawn with the servants portrayed in

Dionisius the Tyrant. It is difficult at this stage to see quite how the plot will develop, but with Felix's employment of a procuress - the sort of old woman warned about by Philips - the real threat arrives. She it is who will play on those very virtues in Paulina which Sachs has been so careful to underline: her tenderness, her loyalty, her loving nature, and her nobility. These she will use to ensnare Paulina, with the help of a poor, sickly puppy. The unsuspecting Paulina is no match for the experienced procuress. Her sympathy is aroused by the sight of the pup, and her trusting nature leads her not to suspect she is being ensnared by lies. A modern audience, accustomed at best to dealing with literary metamorphoses of the sort found in Kafka's works, for example, might find Paulina's believing that the puppy is the procuress's metamorphosed daughter less than credible. In a sixteenth-century world and to a sixteenth-century audience more attuned to witchcraft and spells, the proposition might not seem outrageous. Paulina is led to relate her fidelity to her husband with suffering caused to Felix, and to equate her steadfast loyalty to that of the supposed daughter. She assumes her punishment for causing pain to Felix will be a similar metamorphosis, and agrees to submit to his desires in order to preserve herself in human form for her husband, when he returns. In a world whose values have suddenly been turned upside down by the persuasive procuress, Paulina's fidelity is seen as a sin, her agreeing to sin as her path to salvation. It is enough for Sachs to indicate what the future holds: he does not present Paulina's seduction on stage. The last speech is delivered by the procuress, who boasts of her success in ruining marriages and in arranging for virgins to be deflowered.

At this stage, wholesome values have been seen to be overturned within the play. In the context of carnival, however, with its own world-turned-upside-down order, Sachs does attempt to restore the balance, the proper order of things, to some extent. The final couplet - Sachs's couplet - comes as a blessed relief, as a brief outburst of moral outrage at the prospect of the ruin to be caused to a loving marriage by those who display a cynical disregard both for the institution and for Philips and Paulina personally. Nonetheless, the counterblast to the evil of the procuress and Felix is short and seemingly desperate. Sachs can rarely have left an audience with such a sense of the fabric of society being irreparably damaged, and the innocent being made to suffer, as he does in this drama. It must rank as one of his most powerful and disturbing creations.

The Crying Pup

Enter wife, with ageing nobleman husband:
>   From your boots and spurs, my Lord,
>   I see you mean to travel abroad.
>   Tell me, what is your intent?

Squire:
>   Dearest wife, you know I've spent
> 5   Some time now, as I near old age,
>   Planning one last pilgrimage.
>   You see me now as I depart
>   For the Holy Land, with gladsome heart.
>   Companionship I will not lack,
> 10   For at my front and at my back
>   Ride Bernhardin and Wilhelmo,
>   The closest friends a man could know
>   And noble brothers, full of grace.

Paulina, his wife:
>   Dear husband, will you cross the face
> 15   Of mighty oceans on your way?
>   The thought fills me with sheer dismay.
>   Spare us all this great ordeal!

Squire Philips:
>   God bless you wife! I know you feel
>   Anxiety. But I've arranged
> 20   A holy quest which can't be changed:
>   As my father earned the right,
>   I, too, would become a knight. [1]

Paulina:
>   Since you're leaving me alone -
>   Who will be my chaperone
> 25   To guard my honour? As you know,
>   The world is full of wicked foes,
>   And womankind but poor and weak!

---

[1] Sachs's audience, despite being predominantly drawn from the urban 'middle class' and from the peasantry, would be familiar with chivalric rituals and rites of passage, one of which was the successful undertaking of a pilgrimage to the Holy Land leading to the status of knighthood.

Philips, the squire:
>   I know full well you're not so meek,
>   Paulina! You are chaste and pure:
> 30   In your hands, virtue is secure.
>   But don't trust men with dancing bears,
>   Or wizened crones selling wares!
>   People flatter to deceive.
>   Do what you've done before, and leave
> 35   The world to mourn you for a while.

Paulina, his wife:
>   Well, my Lord, I'll force a smile
>   If you feel you must depart;
>   And wish you, from a loving heart,
>   God speed unto the Holy Land,
> 40   And safe return to where we stand.

They embrace. Exit Philips. Paulina:
>   Well, now my loving husband's gone,
>   I'll concentrate my mind upon
>   A life of quiet abstinence,
>   Foregoing any merriments,
> 45   Until I see him here again.
>   I'll scarce go out, and only then
>   To go to church, to sing and pray
>   For my dear husband far away.
>   Indeed, I hear the gentle pealing
> 50   Of the bells - the Bishop's kneeling
>   Even now at private prayers.
>   I'll join him - this will ease my cares.

Exit Paulina. Felix, a young nobleman, watching her disappear:
>   Philips Balbona has a wife
>   Sweet and tender as is life
> 55   Itself: her gestures full of grace,
>   And Venus herself has no prettier face!
>   When God completed His creation,
>   Paulina was the consummation!
>   With her husband bound for the Holy Land,
> 60   I've time and space to seek her hand;
>   And should my courtship prove in vain,
>   I'll die, and think it worth the pain!
>   My erotic quest will start tonight
>   Outside her home, where I'll delight
> 65   Her with my songs and wistful strings,

To try and make her heart take wing.
And if she looks on me with favour -
There's a thing my heart will savour.
Felix would indeed become
70 The happiest man in Christendom!
The battle-cry for my campaign:
'Nothing ventured, nothing gained'.

Exit. Enter Paulina, carrying a letter:
Felix Spini writes to me
And makes confession, all too free,
75 Of his love. He sings all night,
He races, jousts with all his might -
And just for me! The Devil take him!
I wish no suitor, but can't make him
Cease. My loyal household servants
80 Have kept me safe from all the ferments
Of the outside world - as yet.
This Felix weaves a cunning net,
But he'll never gain my loving favours:
There's only one alive who savours
85 All my love - my husband dear.
Still, Felix inundates me here
With gifts, which I return unseen.
I spurn them - like the go-between
Who came to plead his case: I fear
90 I sent her back with a flea in her ear!

Exit. Enter Felix, the young nobleman, looking sick and speaking sadly:
Doomed from the womb to a life of gloom!
For seeds of hope there is no room
In my heart, now Paulina spurns
My ardent love, whose bright flame burns
95 Undiminished, nonetheless.
Without her, there's no peace or rest.
I neither sleep, nor eat, nor drink.
My heart cries out in pain and sinks,
When faced with her heart's diamond walls.
100 Yet this malady, which so enthralls,
Does not prevent me every day
From making my laborious way
To my love's house, where I wait in vain
To catch a glimpse of her fair frame,
105 Should she happen to appear.
She's all that my poor heart holds dear.

And so the flames of love devour
Felix, who at every hour
Awaits a sad release through death -
110   An end to all his wretchedness.

Enter the old procuress, carrying a long rosary:
To see this young man sitting here,
Sighing and weeping bitter tears,
Moves my heart to tenderness.
I'll try to move him to express
115   Just why he seems so full of woe,
So sick and weak and brought so low.
Young man, what ails you? Tell me do!

Felix, the young nobleman:
I can't and won't reveal to you
The source of my heart's injury.
120   I'll die and end this purgatory!

The old procuress:
My son, don't give way to despair!
If you can bring yourself to air
Your problem, I might ease your plight.

Felix:
A thousand things have failed which might
125   Have cured me of this malady.

The old procuress:
We still have time, if you'll agree.
My comfort and advice are yours.

Felix:
I'll tell you then. I die, because
With every fibre of my soul,
130   With a passion that's beyond control,
I love and court a lady fair:
Paulina, who's beyond compare.
And yet she scorns my poor attempts
To win her; though I joust and fence
135   And write her notes and send her gifts,
My courtesies receive short shrift.
Far from thinking well of me,
Paulina shows hostility,
And angrily has made it clear

140 My attentions are unwelcome here.
But though Paulina makes it plain
That she'll deny my hopes of gaining
Her affection, I can't hate her:
I wander round, hoping sooner or later
145 That I will glimpse my heart's desire.
Yet if by chance it should transpire
That we two meet - she turns her head,
Hurrying away, she cuts me dead.
And so my heart is racked with grief.
150 A yearning pain beyond belief
Embraces it and gnaws away,
Diminishing me day by day.
Once the happiest of men,
Poor Felix now can see no end
155 To misery - unless he save
Himself by hastening to his grave.

The old procuress:

I trust that I can bring you cheer.
You'll find salvation soon appear,
Aided by my shrewd advice -
160 Which does, of course, have its price.
What kind of gift had you in mind?

Felix, giving her some money:

Old woman, here, I hope you find
These sovereigns are enough reward.
And if the outcome should accord
165 With what I wish, and I embrace
Paulina, having won her grace
And favour, I shall be quite cured.

The old procuress:

Your grieving heart may rest assured.
I'll soon bring news - depend on me -
170 To banish your despondency.
The one who scorned and made you suffer
Will soon embrace you as her lover.

Exit Felix. The old procuress:

Now, what I need is a sure campaign
To carry out what I have claimed.
175 The lady's noble, pure, and chaste:
A procuress would surely waste

Her time on her and be thrown out.
I'll need a cunning ruse, no doubt.
Ah! There's a possibility!
180 My little dog might hold the key!
I'll starve him for a day or two,
Then feed him with a tasty brew
Of mustard powder, mixed with broth.
He'll be so hungry that he'll quaff
185 The lot - and then he'll whine and cry.
This shall be my strategy
To trap our proud and noble hind!
I'll pretend that I'm a religious kind,
And talk to her of spiritual things.
190 Such a cunning ruse will bring
Success. But now I must prepare,
And go and set my wicked snare.

Exit the old witch [2]. Enter Paulina:
This suitor just won't be dismissed!
For all my coldness, he insists
195 On promenading every day,
And gaping in a half-mad way
At my house - like some poor sad fish
Who's destined for the serving dish!
And if he yearns himself to death,
200 He'll never hear from me a breath
Of tenderness: my love's reserved
For my husband, whom may God preserve.

Enter the old procuress, carrying a rosary and her puppy:
Noble lady, have no fear,
An errand of mercy brings me here.
205 I'm sent by one who even now
Gives birth to yet another mouth
To feed: she begs a small donation
To save her children from starvation.
Six poor babes upon her hands,
210 No sheep, no cows, no crops, no land,
Her husband just a woodsman plain.
Dear lady, let me say again,
I mean to cause you no offence,

---

[2]This is an interesting and significant change of nomenclature.

> For in this piteous circumstance
215   I come to you in God's own name.

Paulina, handing her half a crown:
> Who could refuse you or complain?
> But, having won my charity,
> Perhaps you could explain to me
> What your trade is, or profession?

The old procuress:
220   Providing helpful intercession.
> For pilgrimages I am paid,
> To Aix or Rome, all of them made
> So others may gain absolution.
> When rich folk die my contribution -
225   At dead of night or break of day -
> Is to kneel beside their bed and pray,
> With my Holy Book and rosary.
> I live a life of charity.

Paulina:
> Then, Lady, would you intercede
230   For my husband, in his hour of need?
> Pray for his swift and safe return
> From the Holy Land, and you will earn
> This sovereign, which I gladly give!

The old woman, taking the money and folding her hands:
> Such gifts enable me to live!
235   In taking this I won't conceal
> It represents the first square meal
> My dog and I have had today.

Paulina:
> He cries in such a piteous way!
> The tears are rolling down his cheeks.

The old woman, folding her hands:
240   I beg of you, don't make me speak,
> Sweet Lady, of the history
> Of how this poor pup came to be
> In such a lamentable state:
> To think of it exacerbates
245   The torment which besets my soul!

Paulina:

> What harm is there if you unfold
> Your story while we're here alone?
> If he's just crying for a bone,
> We'll feed him so he's fit to burst!

The old procuress, in tears:

250   The situation is far worse
> Than that: it touches life and death.
> I weep and struggle to draw breath
> When I think back on the strange events
> Which threaten to rob me of my sense.

255   Soon my pain will grow so great
> That I must face an awful fate.

Paulina:

> I wish you could reveal the truth!

The old procuress:

> This puppy in the Spring of youth -
> I feel I can confide in you -

260   Was once my daughter, fair and true:
> A pious beauty, pure and chaste,
> Who thought it in the poorest taste
> To be the object of desire
> For a young man, who, with heart afire,

265   Wooed her with both gifts and deeds.
> To his courtship she would pay no heed.
> Finding his love rudely scorned,
> The young man deemed the chase forlorn,
> Succumbed to illness, pined away,

270   And died, to everyone's dismay.
> The Goddess Venus, strangely moved
> By the death of one whose love had proved
> So fateful, then devised a plan:
> The metamorphosis began,

275   As punishment for the stubbornness
> Which killed such loving tenderness.
> The little pup here in my arms
> Is my daughter, once so full of charms,
> But now condemned to whine and cry,

280   While her mother's heart is filled with sighs.

Paulina, lamenting:

> Your story, Lady, shocks the ears
> And fills my heart with dreadful fears:
> For I have sinned in just this way,
> Spurning one who has displayed
> 285 For weeks and months a steadfast love.
> I've deemed myself to be above
> Young Felix and his noble passion,
> Treating him in the coldest fashion:
> Rejecting gifts, ignoring favours,
> 290 Shunning all his loving labours,
> Making plain for all to see
> The unwavering fidelity
> My husband merits from his wife.
> Now Felix leads a blighted life,
> 295 Scorned by one he holds so dear.
> Day by day he would appear
> Visibly to waste away,
> His life thrown into disarray.
> What penance should I now perform
> 300 To compensate him for the harm
> I've done? I need your wise advice.

The old procuress:

> I'll make it simple and concise:
> You should long since have been requiting
> This pure love, and not indicting
> 305 Felix for his declaration.
> Should there be no consummation,
> And your hard heart cause his demise,
> Then Venus, winging from the skies,
> Will punish you, as, once before,
> 310 She changed my girl into this poor
> Pathetic pup, condemned to whine
> And whimper till the end of time.
> Unlock your heart! Change your mind!
> Respond! And let young Felix find
> 315 True love. If not.. well, there's my daughter.

Paulina:

> O mother, you have truly taught a
> Vital lesson here today.
> I've learnt that one should not gainsay
> A suitor: chastity is sin!
> 320 Tell Felix that he may begin

184

To reap the fruits of his devotion
And love me freely: my emotions
From now on will be unchecked.
I hope that Venus will respect
325 My change of heart, and that she may
Forgive me. Mother will you stay
With me tonight? You're wise and true,
There's much that I can learn from you.
These sovereigns are a poor reward,
330 But if I offer bed and board
To you and to your crying pup
On Sundays, will you take it up?
Let's talk it over while we share
The supper that I've had prepared.

Exeunt. Enter Felix, the young nobleman, full of joy:
335 Strolling round the town last night
I spied Paulina, who caught sight
Of me: a blush rose to her cheeks,
She made as though she wished to speak,
Then smiled at me with a little pout!
340 I went to bed and dreamt about
Paulina with a heart so light,
And spent a wholly blissful night.

Enter the procuress:
Good day, Sir Felix, and well met!
Your procuress has cast her net
345 And caught the one you deified,
The one for whom you nearly died.
This evening, as the twilight falls,
Find the gate in her garden walls:
Paulina will receive you there
350 And show you joys beyond compare!

Felix, the young nobleman:
The prize is mine! I've won the game!
Take these ten sovereigns for your pains:
A handsome but deserved reward.
My life and health have been restored.
355 My loving arms will soon enfold
That beauty, for so long so cold.
And now Paulina's been obtained,
Felix can live up to his name!

Exit. The old procuress closes the play:

	Procuring women somehow lacks
360	The tedium of spinning flax!
	I keep myself fed and refreshed
	By trading in young female flesh!
	Lacking honour I may be -
	And I've practised my hypocrisy
365	In houses up and down the land -
	But I know my trade like the back of my hand.
	I thrive on cheating, live for lies:
	The Devil's behind my spaniel eyes.
	In cases where Old Nick declines
370	A tricky task, the job is mine.
	And if, through my own indiscretion,
	One day I'm forced to make confession
	Of what I am, the cost to me
	Will be a branding, or the pillory.
375	Decent folk will surely say
	A ducking is the only way
	To rid the world of harmful vermin
	Such as I, and they'll determine
	I should drown like a sack of rats,
380	As punishment for many acts
	Of subterfuge and wickedness,
	Malevolence and lawlessness.
	I've caused no end of marital strife
	And ruined many a virgin's life!
385	'God save the pious from such attacks
	And keep us holy', says Hans Sachs.

Dramatis personae:

Philips Balbona, an ageing nobleman.
Paulina, his wife.
Felix, a young nobleman.
The old procuress.

Anno salutis 1554, on the 25th day of January.

26/1

26/3

7.   *Celebrating the Consecration of the Church at Mögeldorf,*
    Bartel Beham, 1527.

13. THE FARMER CARRYING A FOAL

Ein faßnachtspil mit vier personen
Der schwanger bawer mit dem fül
26 January 1559

With this last play in our selection, Sachs is on familiar territory for
carnival comedy: the world of dim-witted peasants. Moreover, this
particular play does not represent the only occasion in Sachs's carnival
comedies where the mysteries of the reproductive system seem beyond the
grasp of man: one thinks of the *Kelberbruten*, for example, where the lazy,
good-for-nothing husband tries to replace a drowned calf by sitting on a
cheese, in an attempt to make maggots hatch and grow into calves. [1]
Here, in addition, we witness that thematic concentration on other bodily
functions - such as breaking wind, urinating, and defecating - which forms
part of the tradition of the carnival comedy: although Sachs makes far less
use of these topics than earlier writers in the genre. [2] To be strictly
accurate, Cuntz and his wife are not mere peasants: they have their own
farmhand, Heintz, and thus ought to be seen as farmers. Such a nice
distinction would have been unlikely to carry much weight with an urban
carnival audience, though, who knew an accurate generalisation about rural

---

[1]*Faßnacht-spiel mit 3 personen: Das kelberbruten (1551)*, see: Keller and Goetze, Vol.
14, pp. 170-83.

[2]See: E. Catholy, *Fastnachtspiel*, p. 42 ff., and B. Könnecker, *Hans Sachs*, pp. 60-62.

life when they saw it.

We enter *in media res*, with a description of Cuntz's digestive problems, and are afforded what may or may not be a wholly accurate insight into the dietary conditions of the rural poor in winter: root crops and water, greedily wolfed down, are the source of Cuntz's disorder. Immediately, Sachs enhances the realistic tone of the piece with a reference to medical diagnosis by urine testing, a common practice in the Middle Ages and in the sixteenth century. The introduction of Isaac, the potion-selling Jew, also comes in the first two minutes or so of the play: from now on, there is little for Sachs to do but let the plot unfold. It is, however, the arrival of the real dunce of the piece, Heintz, which will lend the plot the necessary comic twist. He it is who gallops off on the old blind mare to take the urine sample to Isaac, drops it, and replenishes the empty bottle with the pregnant mare's urine. The near-aside from Cuntz that any illness which might be shown up by the Jew's 'analysis' could be ruinous, as he has not finished threshing, is not developed by Sachs into a serious socio-economic strand in the text.

Isaac is afforded one of the longest speeches in this play, or indeed in any of the plays in this volume, explaining his colourful background as a trickster, both as a seer and as a healer. His lack of qualifications means he cannot practice inside a reputable town or city: he is forced to make his money from tricking gullible peasants at fairs (and no doubt at shrovetide), convincing them of his credentials with false letters of recommendation and giving them strong purges as 'cures', the best and most effective medicine he knows. [3]

The contest between Isaac and these peasants is as one-sided as that between the wandering student and the farmer and his wife; and, as

---

[3]There is an interesting parallel in Grimmelshausen's works, when Simplex makes a temporary living as a quack doctor. See: H. J. C. von Grimmelshausen, *Der Abentheurliche Simplicissimus Teutsch und Continuatio des abentheurlichen Simplicissimi*, ed. R. Tarot, Tübingen, 1984, pp. 310-16.

is the case with *The Travelling Scholar in Paradise*, Sachs does not allow apparently secondary issues of morality or criminality to disturb the flow of the story and put him off making his point, which is to expose the stupidity of those deceived. This in itself affords us an interesting insight into the whole complex of law and order issues during carnival, where criminal or otherwise disruptive behaviour was often temporarily condoned or passed over in silence, and accepted as one of the hazards of granting a measure of licence to the people.

Having thus far failed to profit from curing the ailments associated with excesses of carnival - Isaac makes direct reference to his potential clients having indulged the previous night in the indiscriminate eating and swilling associated with carnival, though, interestingly, this does not apply to Cuntz - Isaac makes short work of Heintz, the only customer to cross his threshold. But this is not before Sachs indulges in what a modern audience would instantly recognise as run-of-the-mill comic-and-stooge dialogue. This was played, no doubt, direct to the public, almost as a separate entertainment within the play: part of a pattern of such interludes or plays-within-plays which is to be found in Sachs's carnival comedies, and which is certainly represented in the present selection. [4] This quasi-music-hall routine is woven back into the plot as Heintz describes his master's morning stool - an admiring, even loving depiction, but only for those with a strong stomach - and as Isaac announces the miraculous pregnancy. Sachs's audience, then, would have found itself sharing a joke with a quack Jewish healer at the expense of a very stupid rustic: an indication that carnival is a great leveller and a great occasion for ignoring the normal social conventions which would, in another context, have heaped opprobrium on the head of an Isaac. The humour here is akin to that informing the near-anarchic adventures of *Till Eulenspiegel*: just as

---

[4] See Chapter 8, footnote two, p. 112.

malicious, just as invidious, and ultimately just as ineffectual, because the situation depicted is too extreme, too much of a gross caricature of normal experience to form a solid target for satire. [5]

Meanwhile, back at the farm, the waiting couple are given some splendid 'business' as they wait for Heintz to return: the spoon-swallowing scene. Once the news of the supposed pregnancy is out, the climax of the play is reached with Cuntz's panic reaction, his exaggerated birth pangs, his heroic account of his labours, and the eulogy of his first-born stallion - or rabbit, to be more precise. His wife's surmise that her man became pregnant with a foal because of his penchant for eating oats, as horses do, draws her into the tangled web of doltish misinterpretations from which the play derives much of its strength and humour.

The end of the play, rather like the beginning of *Evil Fumes*, harks back to the oldest traditions of carnival and Shrovetide comedies. The action 'on stage' merges or dissolves into real life (or at least, as real as life can be when the context is that of carnival), as Cuntz plans a Shrovetide party with heaps of doughnuts - the eating of 'Krapfen' is still an integral part of carnival - and lots of fun and games: the very circumstances within which the play is being staged. Follies are forgiven and judgement is suspended, as the thin dividing line between actors and audience disappears and all involved in portraying or witnessing the staged events merge as equals in the broader context of carnival celebrations. The play, then, is not about parenthood or gynaecology, nor is it merely designed to mock the gullibility of peasants. It has a broader purpose, which is to unite people in an act of forgiving conviviality.

---

[5] *Ein kurtzweilig Lesen von Dil Ulenspiegel (1515)*, ed. W. Lindow, Stuttgart, 1966.

The Farmer Carrying a Foal

Enter Cuntz Rubendunst, a farmer, with his wife, Gretha:
> Oh wife, my belly's in a state -
> And yet I wasn't drinking late,
> And didn't try that home-made wine
> That makes me fart in double time.
> 5 That's quicker than the strongest purge
> And really makes you feel the urge!
> So tell me, then, what's wrong with me?

Wife:
> Husband, it is plain to see:
> While I sat at the spinning wheel
> 10 Last night, you wolfed down quite a meal
> From that old pile of frozen beet -
> Then drank cold water from the leat.
> I tried to warn you more than once,
> But sometimes you're a proper dunce!
> 15 I knew that I would get no sleep:
> You snorted like a dying sheep
> And ground your teeth the whole night long.

Farmer:
> I knew that there was something wrong,
> So I peed a bit into a glass.
> 20 I was talking only Saturday last
> To Eberlein Grölzenbrey,
> Who told me of a bloke nearby -
> A Jew called Isaac who sells potions.
> I tell you, wife, I've got a notion
> 25 To send our Heintz there with this bottle.

Wife:
> Do it, husband! Not a lot'll
> Go wrong - and its worth the price!
> You're right to seek the Jew's advice:
> Your health's the most important thing.

Farmer:
> 30 Heintz, come in! Stop loitering!

Enter Heintz:
> In the house? Why, what's amiss?

Farmer:

> Take this sample of my piss
> And ride to Sendelbach, post-haste;
> And when you reach the inn, don't waste
> 35 A second: find out straight away
> Where Isaac, the Jewish doctor, stays.
> Bid him, for a modest fee,
> To test this sample of my pee
> And recommend a way to surely
> 40 Cure what's making me feel poorly.
> Take two florins on account.

Heintz, the farmhand, taking the bottle (actually a retort glass) and the money:

> If speed's the thing, I'd better mount
> Our old grey mare - the one that's blind.
> We'll gallop off and quickly find
> 45 The inn, and then locate the Jew,
> And buy a potion, freshly brewed,
> And hurry back at breakneck speed!

Exit Heintz. Wife:

> A little rest is what you need,
> Husband. Wrap up nice and snug.
> 50 I'll go and fill the milking jug
> And feed the cattle in the byre.

Farmer:

> This illness could be pretty dire.
> The threshing's far from over yet -
> I could end up the year in debt!

Exeunt. Enter Isaac, the Jewish doctor:

> 55 I'm Isaac, and it's pretty plain
> I'm just as Jewish as my name.
> I used to claim I was a seer:
> When some poor peasant paid to hear
> The whereabouts of stolen goods,
> 60 Or when I claimed I understood
> The source of fever, pain, and worse,
> Was some strange, secret 'threshold curse'!
> My magic potions speeded healing;
> I made a business of revealing
> 65 Treasure-troves - until exposed!
> And so a different course I chose.

The seer became a medical man,
And thus a new career began!
I've studied no black arts or science:
70   I've learnt my medicine from my clients.
And since I am not qualified,
No decent town lets me inside
Its gates. I have to earn a crust
At country fairs, where I gain the trust
75   Of simple peasants with some letters
Of recommendation from their betters.
They're fakes, of course: it just appears
I've healed the public all these years!
I con them all. The only cure
80   I know to be both quick and sure
Is giving them a good strong purge:
They know it works when they feel the urge!
Some get better, some may die -
By then, I've bid them all goodbye.
85   It's time to take a look outside.
These peasants come from far and wide
Carrying their little glass.
They queue up at my door to ask
If their urine shows up some disease -
90   And then I charge them what I please!

Exit. Enter Heintz:

Today just ain't my lucky day!
Guess what happened on the way
Here. I was trotting on my mare,
Carrying the piss with care,
95   As Sendelbach hove into sight.
The mare - whose day is always night
Because she's blind - trips on a root.
Arse over elbow, off I shoot
And spill the bottle on the ground.
100   I'm lying there, I hear a sound:
The mare is pissing. What a waste!
I fill the bottle up, post-haste!
So now I have to find the Jew,
And get him to inspect this brew.
105   If he's as learned as they say,
He'll see the trouble right away.
If there's a cure, then that's all right;
But if he finds some awful blight
That means my boss must lose his life:

110   Then I'll be free to woo his wife!
Dame Fortune can be most unfair:
She's near as blind as our old mare.
The Jew must be here in the village -
Let's hope if find him without more spillage!

Exit. Enter Isaac:

115   Trade's a little slack today.
Not a soul has made his way
To have his urine checked. This sinner's
Going to have a meagre dinner.
I'll have to take pot luck, or fast,
120   Or fight the cat for the very last
Scraps. And yet it seemed to me
Last night the peasants all made free
With beer and wine - and ate their fill.
And if blood pudding doesn't make them ill,
125   I'll go all day without reward:
A misery I can scarce afford.

Heintz knocks. Isaac:

Who's that with a battering ram?
All right! I'm coming as fast as I can!

Enter Heintz:

Sir, may I bid you a good day!
130   Are you called Flysack, like they say,
Are you the Jew who doctors here?

Isaac:

My name is Isaac, not, I fear,
Flysack. What is your request?

Heintz:

At my master's own behest
135   I've brought for you to have a look -
All the way from Grossenbuch -
This specimen of his fresh pee.
He wants to know if he's diseased.

Isaac, looking at the specimen:

Tell me, where does he feel the pain?

Heintz:

140   At home in bed where he's a-laying.

Isaac:
> I mean, is it a certain member?

Heintz:
> His belly rumbles like September
> Thunderstorms, for days on end.

Isaac:
> Tell me now, my simple friend,
> 145 Does he ever get catarrh?

Heintz:
> He gets his hair cut by his ma!

Isaac, looking again at the specimen:
> Tell me, does he spit and cough?

Heintz:
> Like some volcano going off:
> He coughs and belches flame and smoke!

Isaac:
> 150 It's getting to be beyond a joke!
> So tell me, then, you cheeky pup,
> Is your master all blocked up?

Heintz:
> No, have no fear, that's not the case:
> There aren't no locks at his old place.
> 155 He can come and go at will.

Isaac:
> That wasn't what I asked, but still...
> Is your master growing thin?
> Does he suffer much from wind?

Heintz:
> Oh, he's got wind enough, all right!
> 160 The farm is on a windy site
> And looks a proper wreck at times!

Isaac:
> That wasn't what I had in mind.
> Tell me, does your master fart?

Heintz:

165
Oh yes - he's master of the art.
He let one rip first thing today
That nearly blew the shed away.
The hens flew backwards in alarm
And landed in the threshing barn!

Isaac:

170
Enough! Enough! Now, as a rule,
Does he have a proper stool?

Heintz:

175
But Sir, he's just a simple man
From peasant stock; you'll understand
He's never rightly been to school.
He reads the seasons - and, as a rule,
He's the one who pens the sheep!

Isaac:

This could make a strong man weep!
Does he make a proper stool?

Heintz:

180
Oh yes, he's not an utter fool.
He's made stools, and he's made chairs -
He can sit just where he cares!

Isaac:

That wasn't what I wished to hear!
Now tell me plainly, nice and clear -
Does he use the little room?

Heintz:

185
Aha! I think you may assume
I've caught your drift! Of course he goes
To his little room for a little doze.
He still claims that he's feeling funny:
Weaker than a new-born bunny!

Isaac:

190
I'll ask you plainly - out with it!
Can your master do a shit?
Is my question nice and clear?

Heintz:

Is that all that you want to hear?
Then let me put your mind at ease.
He squats down comfy as you please
195   This morning, out beside the fence,
And lays a whopper - frankincense
It clearly weren't! And full of gristle!
The pigs devoured it clean as a whistle.
If you need some for your doctoring
200   I'm not sure that you'll find a thing!

Isaac:

That's not among the worst of signs.
Now let me try just one more time
To put his water to the test,
And see what cure will work the best.

Looking at the specimen:

205   We're witnessing a miracle!
Your master's pregnant with a foal!
This urine sample is unique -
He must be in his eighteenth week.
I'll help him if he guarantees
210   To take this purge, designed to ease
The passage of his little babe!
But if he won't, then I can't save
His life - the foal will soon grow vast.
Run home - he's got to take it fast!

Heintz, handing Isaac the money:

215   Here, take these florins for your trouble -
I've got to get home at the double!

Exit Heintz with the purge. Isaac:

Well, that was worth a jug of wine
And soup and bread at supper time.
That's the best I'll do today
220   Unless more sick folk come my way.

Exit. Enter Gretha and Cuntz. She is carrying a little red wooden bowl of
soup. Husband:

O wife, my belly's feeling weird.
And where has our Heintz disappeared?
He should have been back long ago.

Wife:

> Come and take a seat. You know
> 225   You ought to get a lot of rest.
> Stay nice and warm: you know, the best
> That you can do is drink this soup.

She passes him a little spoon. He looks at it, angrily:

> Where's my ladle? Where's my scoop?
> This little spoon's no use to me!

Wife:

> 230   Relax, dear husband, don't you see
> The broth itself is nothing great?
> A tiny spoon's appropriate.

The farmer takes a couple of spoonfuls. [The actor simulates swallowing the spoon by dropping it up his sleeve]. Farmer cries out:

> They say bad fortune comes in threes!
> Today's the day its picked on me.
> 235   Was ever there a man so cursed?

Wife:

> From your cries I fear the worst
> Dear husband. Tell me, what is wrong?

Farmer:

> I've swallowed your damned spoon; the prong
> Is half-way down my throat and stuck!
> 240   I don't know how to bring it up.

Wife, slapping him on the back to help the spoon down:

> No need, dear husband, for dismay;
> The problem will soon pass away!

Farmer:

> I shudder at the very notion!

Enter Heintz. Wife:

> Here comes Heintz now with a potion!

Heintz:

> 245   Master, there's no use in hiding
> From you that I bring bad tidings.
> The Jewish doctor sees your piss
> And straight away cries 'What is this?'

And swears an oath you're up the pole!
250   You're carrying a baby foal!

Farmer, seizing his belly:
What was it that I just said?
Misfortune's heaped upon my head.
Am I to give birth to a horse?
This pregnancy can't run its course -
255   A foal can't suckle at my breast!
This bad luck's gone beyond a jest!
Who'll act as midwife at the birth?
I'll be the object of the mirth
And scorn of people far and near.
260   I blame it all on you, do you hear?
And once I'm back upon my feet,
Wife or not, I'm going to beat
You back and blue. My misery
Has reached its peak. If death could free
265   Me, that would be a happy state.

Heintz:
Here, there's no need to rant and prate!
The doctor gave me this strong purge
To help your baby to emerge.
If you can take it right away,
270   You'll feel as fit as yesterday.
The foal just can't afford to grow -
So get it down you in one go!

Farmer, sniffing the purge:
Is it wheaten beer or wine?
As vinegar it might do fine!
275   Oh well, I'll screw my eyes up shut
And pray the stuff can cure my guts.

He swallows it in one and rubs his belly:
Good God! It tastes as rough as Hell -
It's made my belly start to swell
And rumble, and my bowels feel loose.
280   It must be made of witches' juice!
I'm on the point of giving birth!
I need to push for all I'm worth!
Come help me, Heintz, support my head,
And take me to the lambing shed.

Heintz leads him out. Wife:

285 Carrying a foal indeed!
   I never knew a man could breed
   A horse. I hope it comes out quick!
   But how did he get up the stick?
   The only thing of any note -
290 He's always liked to scoff his oats.
   Now that's a food they give to horses;
   So the explanation, then, of course, is
   That is how my man got caught!
   Thank God the pregnancy was short.
295 I've never seen a man so keen
   To drop his baby. I'd have been
   Prepared to pay to ease his pain.
   But here's our Heintz come back again.

Enter Heintz:

   O mistress mine, there was no bother -
300 Your husband has become a mother!
   Your little spoon and the ghastly purge
   Made his bowels start to surge;
   He drops his pants and starts to push,
   When a rabbit hiding in a bush
305 Nearby, and resting from the chase -
   Dozing, as it now felt safe,
   Having given the dogs the slip -
   Leaps up just as your man lets rip!
   Out the stuff all starts to tumble,
310 With a slippy-sloppy farty rumble.
   The rabbit takes off like a shot;
   Your husband, looking round, sees what
   He takes to be his first-born babe,
   And cries to it 'Don't run away!
315 Come suckle at your mother's breast!'
   So, when your husband's had a rest
   And comes back in, let him believe
   He bore a foal and has achieved
   A miracle. Not everyone
320 Can bear a nice four-legged son!
   Keep in mind he'll still be sore!
   Ah! That's him coming through the door.

Enter farmer. Wife:

   Tell me, husband, was it worth
   The pain and worry to give birth

325 To your own foal? And are you seized
With joy? If so, then I am pleased.

Farmer:

I'll tell you wife, I'm just amazed.
I swear to you in all my days
I never saw a foal or colt
330 Run quite as fast - just like a bolt
Of lightning heading for the trees,
While I'm still struggling to my knees.
Believe me, wife, I've seen a few,
But there's no other can outdo
335 My own young foal - he's proved his worth.
There's not a better horse on earth:
Strong as oak and twice as handsome,
He'd be worth a king's own ransom -
If we could catch him. Now, my dear,
340 Don't stand around. Go fetch some beer
And make me up a little couch.
Giving birth's a chore - I vouch
I'll need six weeks till I recover
From the labours of a mother.
345 Tasty food and lots of wine
Might help reduce the healing time!
Then, once I'm feeling hale and hearty,
We shall have a Shrovetide party:
Young and old will celebrate
350 With fun and games and drinking late
And eating doughnuts heaped in stacks!
'Just keep it decent', says Hans Sachs.

Dramatis personae:

Cuntz Rubendunst, a farmer
Gretha, his wife
Heintz, the farmhand
Isaac, the Jewish doctor

Anno salutis 1559, on the 26th January.

BIBLIOGRAPHY

Primary Literature: editions of Sachs's works.

Goetze, E., *Hans Sachs. Sämmtliche Fastnachtspiele [...] in chronologischer Ordnung nach den Originalen* (Neudrucke deutscher Litteraturwerke, 26, 27, 31, 32, 39, 40, 42, 43, 51, 52, 60, 61, 63, 64), Halle, 1880-87.

Keller, A. von, and Goetze, E., *Hans Sachs. Werke*, (Bibliothek des litterarischen Vereins in Stuttgart, 102-06, 110, 115, 121, 125, 131, 136, 140, 149, 159, 173, 179, 181, 188, 191, 193, 195, 201, 220, 225, 250), Tübingen, 1870-1908.

Primary literature: translations of Sachs's works.

Anonymous, *A True Description of All Trades; published in Frankfort* [sic] *in the year 1568, with six of the illustrations by Jobst Amman*, Brooklyn, 1930.

Anonymous, *A True Description of All Trades. First published in the year 1568. With six of the illustrations relating to the art of printing by Jobst Amman*, Eugene, Oregon, 1939.

Atkins, H. G., *The Farmer in Purgatory, translated from the German of Hans Sachs - Der Bauer im Fegfeuer, 1552; and The Student in Purgatory*, London, 1926.

Chambers, W. H. H., *Raising the Devil: a Shrove-tide or Carnival Play (Der farent schueler mit dem deufel pannen; ain Fasnacht Spil of Hans Sachs, translated by W. H. H. Chambers*, in A. Bates, *The Drama*, London, 1903.

Clark, I. E., *Hans Sachs: The Narrenschneiden. A Mardi-gras Play.* Translated from the German by I. E. Clark (no date, no place of publication).

Eliot, S. A. Jr., *The Wandering Scholar from Paradise. A Fastnachtspiel with Three Persons,* adapted by S. A. Eliot Jr., in *Little Theater Classics*, Vol. 4, Boston, 1922, and also in B. H. Clark (ed.), *World Drama*, New York, 1933.

Ellis, F. H., *Das walt got: a Meisterlied*. With Introduction, Commentary, and Bibliography [and Translation] by F. H. Ellis *(Hans Sachs Studies*, 1), Bloomington, 1941.

Hunter, B. A., *Who'll Carry the Bag? A Comedy after the Kremerkorb of Hans Sachs*, 1950 (no place of publication).

Krumpelmann, J., *Brooding Calves: Shrovetide Play with Three Persons*. Translated from the German by John Krumpelmann, *Poet-Lore* xxxviii, 1927.

Leighton, W., *Merry Tales and Three Shrovetide Plays by Hans Sachs, now first done into English verse*, London, 1910.

Morgan, B. Q., *The Scholar Bound for Paradise; The Merchant's Basket; The Hot Iron. Three Shrovetide Comedies translated from Hans Sachs*, Stanford University (Microfilm), 1937.

Ouless, E. U., *Seven Shrovetide Plays, translated and adapted from the German of Hans Sachs*, London, 1930.

Ouless, E. U., *The Children of Eve: a Morality*. Translated and adapted by E. U. Ouless, in C. M. Martin (ed.), *Fifty One-Act Plays*, London, 1934.

Rifkin, B. A., *The Book of Trades. Ständebuch*. [Woodcuts by] *Jost Amman and* [text by] *Hans Sachs. With a new Introduction by B. A. Rifkin*, New York, 1973.

Scoloker, A., *A goodly dysputacion betwene a Christen shomaker / and a Popysshe parson with two other parsones more, done within the famous Citie of Norembourgh*, London, 1524.

Wayne, P., *The Strolling Clerk from Paradise, by Hans Sachs. English by Philip Wayne*, in P. Wayne, *One-Act Comedies*, London, 1935.

Other primary texts

Grimmelshausen, H. J. C. von, *Der Abentheurliche Simplicissimus Teutsch und Continuatio des abentheurlichen Simplicissimi*, ed. R. Tarot, Tübingen, 1984.

- *Lebensbeschreibung der Erzbetrügerin und Landstörtzerin Courasche*, ed. W. Bender, Tübingen, 1967.

Opitz, M., *Buch von der deutschen Poeterey*, ed. R. Alewyn (Neudrucke deutscher Literaturwerke, Neue Folge 8), Tübingen, 1963.

Pauli, J., *Schimpf und Ernst*, ed. J. Bolte, 2 vols, Berlin, 1924.

Tydeman, W., *Four Tudor Comedies*, Harmondsworth, 1984. (Contains N. Udall, *Roister Doister*, and W. Stevenson, *Gammer Gurton's Nedle*.)

Secondary Literature

Bastian, H., *Mummenschanz: Sinneslust und Gefühlsbeherrschung im Fastnachtspiel des 15. Jahrhunderts*, Frankfurt, 1983.

Beare, M., *Hans Sachs Selections*, University of Durham, 1983.

Brandt, A.-K., *Die 'tugentreich fraw armut'. Besitz und Armut in der Tugendlehre des Hans Sachs (Gratia, 4)*, Göttingen, 1979.

Catholy, E., *Fastnachtspiel* (Sammlung Metzler, 56), Stuttgart, 1966.

Cramer, T. and Kartschoke, E., *Hans Sachs - Studien zur frühbürgerlichen Literatur im 16. Jahrhundert* (Beiträge zur älteren deutschen Literatur, 3), Bern, 1978.

Dülmen, R. van, and Schindler, N. (eds), *Volkskultur. Zur Wiederentdeckung des vergessenen Alltags (16.-20. Jahrhundert)*, Frankfurt, 1984.

Habel, T., *Brecht und das Fastnachtspiel. Studien zur nicht-aristotelischen Dramatik (Gratia, 3)*, Göttingen, 1978.

Po-Chia Hsia, R. (ed.), *The German People and the Reformation*, Ithaca and London, 1988.

Hughes, M., *Early Modern Germany*, London, 1992.

Kartschoke, E. See Cramer, T. (above).

Könnecker, B., *Hans Sachs* (Sammlung Metzler, 94), Stuttgart, 1971.

Krause, H., *Die Dramen des Hans Sachs. Untersuchungen zur Lehre und Technik*, Berlin, 1979.

Müller, M. E., 'Bürgerliche Emanzipation und protestantische Ethik. Zu den gesellschaftlichen und literarischen Voraussetzungen von Sachs' reform-atorischen Engagement', in T. Cramer and E. Kartschoke, *Hans Sachs* (above).

Schade, R. E., *Studies in Early German Comedy 1500-1650*, Columbia, South Carolina, 1988.

Schütte, J., 'Was ist unser freyhait nutz / wenn wir ir nicht brauchen durffen. Zur Interpretation der Prosadialoge', in T. Cramer and E. Kartschoke, *Hans Sachs*, (above).

Scribner, R., 'Reformation, carnival, and the world turned upside down', *Social History* 3, iii, 1978. Also in R. van Dülmen and N. Schindler, *Volkskultur*, (see above).

Spriewald, I., *Literatur zwischen Hören und Lesen. Wandel von Funktion und Rezeption im späten Mittelalter; Fallstudien zu Beheim, Folz und Sachs*, Berlin and Weimar, 1990.

Wedler, K., *Hans Sachs*, Leipzig, 1976.